NICE TO F#UCK YOU

MONTGOMERY QUINN

Nice To F#ck You

Montgomery Quinn

I'd Like to thank my wonderful Supporters. Thank you for
your contributions to my work

ben r.
daniel
kalli b. j.
ibr88
lejunior
max v.
mike
sithams
william o.
bas s.
bugsy b.
curtiss c.
david c.
kirill l.
lem
michael y.
mike d.

SPECIAL THANKS

moose
philip77
shan w.
sir2319

Thank you for your generosity, feedback and kindness. And
if you'd like to see your name here, check me out on Twitter
for links!
@Monty_Quinn

CHAPTER ONE

J ames Kirk,

WE ARE WRITING to you today, to inform you your services are no longer required. Please return all company property by close of business. Your final pay will be sent out on the usual roster.

WISHING you well
Donna Lee - Head of HR

JAMES JUST SIGHED as he read the email for the fifth time. It wasn't bad enough that he was getting fired. It was that he was an unpaid intern, who'd been assured by Donna at the last meeting that they were hiring him at the end of the following week. So, after shutting down his work computer, packing the few belongings he gave a shit about, James dropped his ID on the desk and got up. There was no need to say goodbye on the way out. He hadn't been there long enough for anyone but the attractive receptionist to have remembered his name.

"James, where do you think you're going?" A voice snapped.

James slowed and sighed softly to himself. "Home Donna, I'm going home."

"Home?" She frowned, "It's noon James."

"Yeah well," he shrugged and started heading for the door. "Sposee you can just dock my pay then."

"This is highly unprofessional!" She snapped, storming after him.

"Unprofessional," James laughed. By now he had the attention of the entire room. "How about we compare the minutes from our last meeting, where you told me you were going to hire me next week, and compare it to the email you just sent me, saying I was fired?"

James shook his head and kept walking, even as Donna gaped in astonishment behind him.

"Is it true?" Alice asked as he passed by reception.

James nodded, "Yeah. It was lovely to meet you."

"You too," she smiled.

Pushing open the door, James stepped outside and took a deep breath. Then realising how shitty the air quality was in the city, he sighed and headed for his car. The beat up old Corolla didn't look like much, but it started and ran without any issues. And it had done so since his dad gifted it to him when he first decided to move to the city.

"Is this really what I want?" James asked himself out loud, as he dropped his stuff on the passenger seat and started the car.

Turning back to the office, he saw Alice wave sadly at him. With a quick wave of his own, James started driving.

Swinging into the apartment his parents rented for him, James found himself staring at the walls. It was dank, empty and was barely more than a place to sleep. Just a bedroom, a small kitchen and a shower with a toilet. It was the cheapest thing he could find that his parents were willing to pay for while he got on his feet. And now his biggest shot was over.

KNOCK KNOCK

James frowned, before getting up and heading for the door. Checking through the peephole, all he could see was the uniform for a courier service. Pulling the door open, James frowned at the young man who smiled back.

"You've probably got the wrong place," James told him.

The young man frowned for a moment and checked the thick cardboard envelope in his hand. "James Kirk?"

"Ummm…" James paused, "Yeah, actually."

"Great, sign here," the young man handed over a small tablet device and waited as James put his signature on it.

Then James was left staring at the oversized envelope. It had no name, or return address. So he sighed and pulled the tab. Prying open the envelope, he tipped it up and out slid a key with a note. James examined the ordinary looking key for a moment, before checking the note.

James,

IF YOU ARE READING THIS, *congratulations of the change of lifestyle. My time has come and now it is yours.*

You'll know what to do

UNCLE JAMES

P.s. Don't get rid of the cupid statue

P.p.s seriously don't
P.p.p.s seriously, seriously don't, like promise me right now!
P.p.p.p.s give your old man a hug, he won't take this well

JAMES READ THE NOTE TWICE. One one side of things, the death of his uncle was devastating, their family had always been close. Close to the point James was named after the man. It had been a couple years since he'd had time to visit. Uncle James had run a spa retreat in the mountains near their home town. It was widely popular in the past and James always loved the relaxed atmosphere. Frowning for a moment, James checked the envelope and he was glad he did. The note had fallen out, but there was still a wad of paper-work in there. Pulling it out, James gasped, reading the ownership paperwork, saying he was now the owner of the spa.

Pulling out his phone, James searched for the correct Matthew for his father. It rang twice before answering.

"Hey son," he answered softly

"I'm sorry dad," James replied.

His father sighed and sniffed, trying to hold back the tears. "He told me y'know. Always said it would happen. And that he'd leave it all to you."

"You know about this?"

"Yeah," his father sighed. "So what are you gonna do?"

This time James sighed, "Well, I have the paperwork that says I own a spa. And my day job just fired me so-"

"What?!" His father yelled.

"Yeah," James groaned. "No idea, last week they were talking about a contract, today, I got an email and well... suppose I'll call this a win?"

"Break the lease son. I'll see you when you get here."

Without a word, James was left holding a phone making

that awful hangup tone. So after hanging up himself, he started packing. It was just like his father. No nonsense when it came down to it. Wasn't worth a goodbye, he knew James was coming. He'd be stupid not to be. It didn't take him all that long. Cleaning out the bathroom took a whole five minutes. All his clothes were still in a suitcase. The laptop he had went back in its bag. The final thing was just the single mattress. It took a little effort, but some time and elbow grease and even it was strapped to the roof. It wasn't the classiest thing he'd ever done, but it was efficient. With a word to the landlord to let him know what was going on, James started driving.

He made a single stop along the way for the bathroom and snacks, before pulling into his parents driveway. By the time James was out of the car, the front door was open and his parents were coming towards him.

"Hey dad," Jame said, accepting a hug from the older man. Then he kissed his mother's cheek, earning him a beaming smile.

"Your room is how you left it," she smiled. "But I don't think you'll use it for more than the night."

James paused in thought for a moment, before remembering the spa had a hotel attached and Uncle James probably just lived there as well.

"Come on. You must be hungry and we can go see the place tomorrow," his father smiled sadly.

With his belly full and his parents blessing, James found an old comfort, falling asleep in his childhood bed.

The following day, James drove his old corolla behind his parents SUV. They'd agreed with his assessment that he'd probably be staying for a while. The drive itself only took an hour. It was like a new world out here. The city long behind, all that was around, was the beauty of the trees and the silence it could bring. James smiled, seeing the old log buildings. They were designed to fit in with the natural surrounds, despite being kept modern on the inside. Nobody wanted to come for a winter spa treatment, then stay in a draughty room. Still, as they drove up to the front doors James could see things had been let go. The trees weren't pruned, the grass was a little long and everything looked like it needed a good paint. Under the front where a ring road was manned by a concierge. The smartly dressed man stood tall and proud as we pulled up.

He waited as we got out, before approaching us. "Would you happen to be the family of Mr Kirk?"

"That would be us," Matthew nodded. "This is my wife, Carla, and my son… James."

The concierge nodded politely and shook hands with both of James's parents, before pausing at the younger man. "Your uncle told us a bit about you. He said you were studying business, but was good with your hands."

James smiled and nodded. "Yeah, Uncle James taught me a few things. I was never his equal, but I was able to pull off a back rub in a pinch."

The man smiled. He was middle aged, a little older than James's father. He was greying at the temples, but had a roguish glint in his eye. When he smiled, it was like a kindly older gentleman and James found himself liking him.

"Right, well I'm glad you're all here. Matthew, Carla, I will show you to your rooms for the time being. James, if you'd like to wait here at reception. I'll be back shortly. We have a bit of paperwork to go over.

"That's fine," James smiled.

"Great, Matthew, Carla, if you'll follow me?"

James followed behind his parents into reception, before peeling off and looking around. The room was the same as it ever was. Large, open, quiet, with plain, relaxing colours and plenty of light, if a bit old and musty smelling. The greeters desk at the far wall was simple, but ornate. And behind that, was the cupid statue. It was something James wondered about. His uncle had spent so much time polishing it and keeping it pristine. There was even a perspex cover over the top. Speaking of…

James stepped around the desk seeing the cover set aside. He moved to pick it up, before noticing a fine layer of dust over the statue. So with a shrug, James turned and checked the cabinet underneath. As expected were some cleaning supplies that looked perfect for the job. Straightening, James gave the statue a quick spray. It was made of bronze and beneath the dust, it gleamed brightly after all the years of being polished. The statue was… odd. It was a cupid, but as if the cupid was more like Hercules. Instead of a little chubby baby holding a bow, it was a musclebound, naked hunk. He stood tall and proud, flexing his body as he pulled back a powerful looking war bow. The other thing of notice was the statue's rather large… Package… James tried not to think about it as he ran the cloth over the surface. If he didn't look, he wasn't touching a bronze dong and that's how he liked to think about it.

Continuing the process of spraying and wiping, James made sure to get it all up to scratch. The bow was the hardest as he had to be careful around all the fine details. It would do no good to have dust trapped under the fingers, or around the arrowhead where it almost touched the hand.

"Thank you James," the concierge said.

James, not hearing the man approach, jumped, before yelping in pain.

"Ouch!"

He felt the sharp jab of the arrow in the side of his finger and it throbbed madly. For just a split second, a jolt of pain ran from his finger, right into his chest, making him think the arrow had been poisoned or something. After a couple beats of his heart the pain stopped.

"James, sir? Are you okay?"

Glancing down at the tiniest pin prick on the side of his finger, James nodded. "Yeah, sorry. Didn't realise how sharp the arrow was and got my finger."

"My apologies," The man smiled widely. "Sir, if you follow me, I'll take you to your uncle's office. There, we have a little paperwork to go over."

"Right," James nodded, checking the small red dot on his finger.

Following behind the concierge, James realised he didn't even know the man's name. Before he could pluck up the courage to ask, the man led him into a familiar looking room.

"Now, you best take a seat on your side," he smiled.

James frowned for a moment, before stepping around to sit at the desk. It was an odd feeling sitting where his uncle sat for all those years.

"Where would you like to begin?"

James blinked for a moment, "Ummm… Your name?"

The concierge smiled. "Call me Baal."

"Baal?" James pondered for a moment. "Like the fertility god?"

"Exactly," Baal smiled.

James eyed the man for a moment, but went along with it. "Alright Baal, what's the plan?"

"Oh this is going to be so much easier," Baal smiled. "Your uncle was a brilliant man, but he was never quite onboard with everything I had to say."

James frowned for a moment, but before he could speak, a rapid set of knocks on the door caught both their attention. Baal glanced at James and James swallowed, realising this was HIS office.

"Come in!"

The door burst open and a young woman stood there. "Oh, I ummm."

"It's fine," James smiled.

The woman looked rather confused as she glanced from James to Baal and back, but settled on a point between them. "Mary closed her finger in a door. She's out to see a doctor and we have nobody to take care of Ms Brown."

James frowned for a moment, "We don't have anyone else on staff to cover?"

The woman seemed to blanch for a moment, but Ball cleared his throat. "Sir, with the death of your uncle. We cut all unnecessary clients and sent most of the staff home with pay. Only those who were considered VIP's were kept on. We could get someone else in, but it would take time."

"You don't-"

"No sir," Baal shook his head. "I greet the clients and book them in. I've never laid my hands on them."

James sighed for a moment, before looking up at the young woman. "Alright, let's see what I can remember from my uncle's training."

"I can't believe this," Margaret Brown grumbled to herself. "First the kids leave for college, leaving me with that two timing bastard. Then he packs up and leaves too. I splurge on the VIP treatment on this shitty little spa, and the first man to touch me in years ups and dies, and there's no replacement."

She was sitting, naked on a bench seat, before the massage table. Even it looked dated. The padding was solid, but worn in places. It hadn't been the most comfortable thing she'd ever laid on, including her soon to be ex-husband.

James, the man who ran this resort, his hands were magical. They hit every spot and left her feeling like a pile of goo on the table. It was the only reason she put up with the dusty room and the rattly air-conditioner. And here she was, waiting for a second taste, only to find out that the man had died, and the replacement had injured herself and wasn't coming. A soft knock on the door snapped her head up.

"It's open," she snapped grumpily. The door swung open, and she froze. "James?" But she quickly realised it wasn't him.

"Ummm," James paused. "Yes and no. Would you like to put something on?"

The woman squeaked and grabbed a towel, covering her breasts. She wasn't ashamed of herself, and had it been James, she'd have appreciated him seeing her. But... "Yes and no?" She asked, covering for her embarrassment.

James nodded. "Yes, I AM James, but I'm not THE James. My uncle passed rather suddenly and... Well it appears I've inherited this place."

Ms Brown softened her expression for a moment. "I'm sorry. I know a little of loss these days. I'd be happy to postpone."

James smiled at the attractive older woman and felt an uncomfortable twinge in his pants. "No, you're here now. I'll refund your visit, but we'll see if I can get you comfortable if you like. I'm not quite my uncle and I'm a bit rusty, but the man did train me."

She smiled and nodded. "Right well..."

"Oh!" James blushed and quickly darted back out of the room.

Ms Brown sighed. He wasn't James. He was cute though, so she could fantasize regardless. As he closed the door, she quickly dropped the towel and got comfortable on the bench. "I'm decent!" she called, settling her face into the mould.

The door opened a few seconds later as James stepped

into the room. He'd been in this position before. Beautiful naked woman, face down on the table. Her ass curved nicely and he swallowed, feeling his pants grow tight. Shaking his head to clear the thoughts, James plastered a professional smile on his face. "Alright Ms Brown. What can I do for you today?"

"I'm still feeling pretty good from my last appointment. And if you're giving me a refund, how about just practice? I'll let you know if something is working or not and you get yourself back in the swing of things."

James smiled and nodded, before realising she couldn't see him. "That sounds perfect then."

Checking the bench at the far side, James flicked the button for the music. Soft tones filled the room and Ms Brown seemed to relax a little further. The oils were kept in a warm bath on a nearby shelf and James examined them. "Any particular scent?"

"Something floral?"

James checked the labels and spotted the one he needed. Plucking it out, James made his way over, before popping the lid and offering it for her to smell.

"Perfect," she purred.

James smiled to himself and got to work. Pouring some oil on his hands and some more over her skin, he spent a few minutes just rubbing her down. The whole time, he paid attention to the tightness of the muscles in her back. He felt the small knots that were forming and built up an idea of how to deal with them. He was completely unaware of how Ms Brown squirmed beneath his fingers.

She, on the other hand, was dying inside. His hands were magical. His uncle had been the first man to put his hands on her. He'd barely begun and she was already trying not to squirm. She could feel the heat building between her legs and despite her embarrassment of leaving a possible wet patch on the table, she found herself wanting more. As his hands began to press and prod, she let out a small moan of pleasure.

James heard the moan and sighed in relief that he was doing something right. He felt around and used the sides of his hands to spread out the pressure as he manipulated the sore muscles under her skin. He tried his best to be as efficient as possible. Not wanting to bruise or cause any pain, but at the same time to relieve her stresses. Whatever had been bothering her had left her tense all over and James found himself wanting to relieve that. As he worked, he lulled himself into a trance. Knowing what he was doing, he kept at it, smoothing away her aches and pains in a world of his own.

Ms Brown was biting her lip. Every spot that ached, he rubbed. Every place that strained he pressed. Every knot was loosened and every pain was eased. As she tried desperately not to moan like the whore her husband referred to her as, Ms Brown couldn't help but want to anyway. His hands drifted over her ass, massaging the firm globes. He passed over them briefly as he moved down each leg, but on his way back up, she imagined the ache in her pussy. She fantasied so deeply about the feeling of his hands touching between her legs. Part of her wanted to ask. A bigger part wanted her to beg. She opened her mouth to say something, anything, but the words wouldn't come out. A firm hand suddenly pushed between her thighs and muscular fingers rubbed along her labia, making her freeze in place.

James slammed back into reality. His hand was pinned, extremely hot and extremely slick. Ms Brown was shaking slightly and making noises. Retracting his hand, James was almost hyperventilating. He was going to jail. He'd been here one day, and now he was going to be arrested and charged.

"I'm so sorry," he said softly. "I have no idea what came over me."

Taking a deep breath and getting ready to call the police himself, he froze as she took a shuddering deep breath. "It's fine, James. Let's... Just finish this off then."

She gingerly rolled over, cringing when she felt the wet mess on the table squelch under her ass. She laid back, before realising she was once again completely naked. The fine, trimmed, patch of pubic hair stuck up, slicked in place from her own juices. James, without a moment's hesitation quickly covered her lower half with a towel.

"I... Um... Are you sure?" James asked.

Ms Brown took a few deep breaths, "Yes James. Please continue."

Nodding, James got the oil ready again. Before applying some to his hands and her stomach. Her breasts sat naturally to each side and he gulped, trying not to think about them. He'd already practically assaulted her once already and she was kind enough to give him a pass. With unsteady hands, James began rubbing the oil into her front. He started at her stomach, then went higher, careful not to touch her breasts directly, as he moved up around her neck and shoulders.

"James?"

He froze.

"You're missing a couple spots," she said softly, keeping her eyes closed.

James cleared his throat with a small cough. "Right... I wasn't sure..."

"It's fine," she said a little quicker than even she thought was necessary. She didn't know why she felt like this, but his hands on her felt amazing. She wanted more and despite the obvious, she couldn't understand why she wanted it quite so badly.

James ignored how Ms Brown bit her lip as his hands

began to rub oil into her breasts. He was gentle, but firm. Making sure he could feel the muscle beneath for problems. Then he got to work. Moving around, he rubbed her stomach, shoulders and yes, even her breasts. Completely unaware of how she rubbed her thighs together as he worked himself into a trance.

Without giving her more than a quick smile, James flicked up a towel, exposing one of her legs, and quickly moving down. Ms Brown groaned, feeling his hands moving along the tops of her thighs. Her pussy throbbed as the tips of his fingers moved so close to her most sensitive place. He tried to remain professional, keeping as much distance as possible. By the time he'd massaged down to her calf and back up, she could feel her own wetness spreading beneath her. He paid it no mind, as he swapped sides and started moving down her other leg.

"James?" she practically whimpered, as his hands finally came off her skin.

James froze, "Yes Ms Brown?"

Thoughts of her cheating husband flashed through her mind. Was this just revenge? She couldn't be sure that wasn't part of it. But the truth remained, her pussy was desperate and it had been a very long time since someone had made her feel like this. "James, there's one part of me you missed."

James's eyes bulged out of his head as she pulled the towel away and spread her legs. Her engorged labia practically drooled onto the table beneath. She held perfectly still as she had before.

"Ummm."

"Please?" She whimpered softly. "It feels so tender."

"Ms Brown..."

"I need this James," she whispered. "Please?"

James gulped, then nodded. He leaned over her and pressed his hands to the insides of her thighs. As he moved his hands up, he built a small picture of the structure beneath the skin. He knew of the discomfort she felt and could feel the tense feeling between her legs. Running his thumbs up each side of her labia, she gasped and rolled her hips. It also became quickly apparent that this was extremely uncomfortable for him.

"I'm going to get up on the table," James said softly, "Move your legs aside so I can work on you better."

Ms Brown was chewing her lip frantically as she followed his instructions. She swung her knees off the sides of the table. Allowing her arms to swing off as well, she lay open and exposed to him. She imagined her arms and legs tied together, so she would be stuck in this position. Open and exposed as his wonderful hands went back to work between her legs. His thumbs ran up and down her labia, making her twitch and gasp. He changed technique, massaging over her mons, making her clit tingle. That led to him pinching her vagina between his fingers, making her labia pout slightly. The firm pressure on her clit made her mind race.

Flexing her kegels reflexively, the small movement seemed to tug beautifully on her clit making her gasp. In return, James rolled his thumb and forefinger, massaging her entire external sex in one action. Ms Brown felt a build up within her as he went. The more she writhed, the more the massage built her pleasure. As her pleasure built, she flexed her kegels, feeling that tiny jerking sensation on her clit that pushed her ever higher. Gasping and sighing, the sensation became a feedback loop as her kegels took on a life of their own, clenching and spasming as he rolled her labia in his fingers until finally.

"Oh fuck!" She squealed.

A massive ball of heat exploded inside her, sending waves of bliss pulsing through her body, starting from her clit. Ms Brown cried out and thrust her hips forward. The sudden, violent pressure of James's hand still pinching, but now rubbing her entire crotch pushed her over the edge. For the first time in years, a squirt of girl-juice sprayed out, soaking the young man. Instantly, she remembered doing that to her husband when they first got together. He'd hated it and gone to wash his face. Ms Brown's anxiety began to peak as she opened her eyes to look for a towel.

So she was caught completely unaware as James's mouth moved down until his mouth made contact with her clit.

He was the most turned on he'd ever felt. All these strange urges and sensations that ran through his body, James just couldn't contain himself. As she squirted, the scent of her filled him entirely and he just had to taste. Releasing her labia from the small massage, he leaned in and gently took her clit in his mouth. The sensation made her jump, but that turned to a squeal when he lightly sucked on it. He didn't want to overstimulate her and kept to a gentle pressure. Her legs shook violently, like she wanted to snap them closed over his head. James decided to lean on them, with his forearms to make sure he had the access he did.

Ms Brown laid there, holding her open mouth as James pinned her legs open. Even if she wanted to close them, she didn't have the strength to lift them onto the table while James pinned her down. Writhing and arching her back, she cried silently as his tongue gently began to lap at her folds. She'd always been sensitive and had enjoyed oral on the odd occasion, but this was otherworldly. As she began to shudder into her second orgasm, she gasped as the sensation vanished, leaving her pussy feeling suddenly cold and empty. Opening her eyes, she caught him looming overhead and nodded.

James felt like the voice in the back of his head. Sure, he was still in control, but his desire had taken over. This beautiful, refined, older woman was desperate for him. He didn't know how he knew, he just knew. Staring down into her doe-eyed expression, James pressed his mouth to hers and pushed his cock inside her at the same time. Ms Brown moaned softly into his mouth. She enjoyed the taste of herself on his mouth, as much as she enjoyed the feeling of his cock stretching her more than her husband ever had. The weight of him on her pelvis forced her legs to stay open, and she wished desperately that she was tied down like in her fantasy. Her core tensed again and she trembled, feeling her second orgasm build.

"In me," she begged softly. "Please, inside. I want to feel you leak out of me for days."

James's lizard brain was in full control. Kissing her fiercely, Ms Brown clutched at him while he slammed his cock into her with all his might. As her pussy muscles began to rhythmically pulse around his cock, James buried himself to the hilt and filled her up. The pulsing, milking sensation of her pussy muscles had him groaning in pleasure, long after the spurts of his thick seed had ended. And he was left staring into the shiny, weepy eyes of a woman old enough to be his mother.

"I'm sorry," James said, seeing the expression on her face. "I didn't mean to hurt you."

Her expression twisted and broke as she burst out laughing. "Hurt?" She giggled. "Oh James, that was fantastic!"

He grinned sheepishly for a moment, before she kissed him firmly. She pulled away, and pushed his head down to lay on her chest as she caught her breath.

"Hey, ummm... Probably the wrong time to ask this, but..."

"Hysterectomy," she said, a tad bitterly. "After my husband got two out of me, he convinced me to get the snip. Now they're all grown up and he's sleeping with his secretary... I feel kinda cheated."

"Is..." James frowned.

"Don't even think it buster," Ms Brown bopped him on the nose. "The idea of an attractive man putting his hands on me, paid my fees. Having you put your hands on me, is the reason I'll be coming back at some point. But... What you just did to me... If you were ten years older..."

James grinned and shuffled a little to get comfortable. The feeling of her pussy around his cock, and her small gasp, told him he was still hard, and still able to continue.

"You're still inside me," she said softly.

"Ummm," James mumbled.

"I've got somewhere to be at three o'clock. So if you can get me in the shower by two, I'm yours until you can't get it up any more."

James sat up, kissed her, and pulled back.

"It would be my pleasure, Ms Brown.

"Call me Maggie," she smiled. "In fact, I want you to scream it."

CHAPTER TWO

The scent of Maggie's skin was still on James's mind as he stepped back into his office. James had never felt this way before. Not in a 'madly in love with an older woman he'd barely met' kind of way. But in a, 'I am so physically turned on, I will fuck you for two hours straight until we both lose track of how many orgasms we've had, and yet still, right now, I could go again,' kind of way. It had even continued in the shower. Maggie's legs by the end shook and she giggled as James helped scrub her down. Before succumbing to their lust as he took her hard against the shower wall one last time. In the end, Maggie had shyly checked their surroundings in reception, given him a toe curling kiss, and promised to come back soon. And with a rather bemused expression, James froze at the sight of Baal, giving him a shit eating grin from the chair where they left off.

"Have fun?"

James swallowed nervously. "Mag-Ms Brown is to get a refund for her visit due to the situation not being what she paid for. She will however be in touch for her next booking."

Ball grinned even wider somehow, "Is that all?"

James tried to stop the blush he felt forming and kept his voice steady. "If we have an automatic VIP list, I want her added to it."

"Oh you're so much easier to deal with than your dear uncle," Ball let out a big whoosh of air.

James frowned, "What do you mean? My uncle built this place."

Baal's smile dropped, "Yes, I'm sorry. There's a bit more to it. But we ran out of time to explain the situation."

James nodded and took a seat behind the desk. "Well we have a bit of time now don't we?"

"We should, yes," Baal smiled. "I put your parents in a suite for the night, by the way. You should join them for dinner and I've asked a couple of the girls to come in tomorrow to give them a morning to relax."

"Speaking of, is there any reason we shouldn't reopen back to normal capacity?"

Baal shook his head, "Not really. But I'd recommend giving it a couple days. Get the funeral over with first. Then open the place up. We can afford to close for a few days."

"How do you know the finances?" James asked.

"It's not my favourite thing here. We used to have someone, but… That didn't work out and your uncle was hopeless with a checkbook."

James smirked, thinking of all the times they went out for ice cream and came back with a plethora of flavours to try. Those were some of his fondest memories. "Right, so what do I need to know?"

Hours later, James slumped into a seat opposite his parents. The dining room was empty of everyone but Baal and whoever was in the kitchen.

"How are you settling in, son?"

James sighed, "Not great dad… Not great."

"James did say things hadn't been going smoothly. How bad is it?" His mother asked.

"The company is almost broke. Maintenance has been backing up. Only a skeleton staff still work here and most of those were sent home when Uncle James passed," he sighed.

"Well we've booked the funeral home," his father sighed. "They're cremating him the day after tomorrow."

James nodded, "I suppose I'll use tomorrow to get this place tidied up then. I'll get Baal to ring all the staff and invite them to the funeral."

"That would be best," his father smiled sadly. "He was well liked by the few people we've met here."

When Baal came out with their meals, the family sat quietly and ate. It was a simple fair, just steak and vegetables. It was good and it hit the spot with the small family. Afterwards, Matthew and Carla went back to their rooms, and James made his way to his office. Pushing open the door, he jumped at the sound of a terrified squeak.

A woman was sitting in his chair and she leapt to her feet. Her expression went wide and happy, before she frowned deeply. "Who are you?! You shouldn't be here!" She snapped.

James blinked as she berated him. She wore a woolen cardigan, over a blue top and skin tight jeans that left little to the imagination. Even as her silver hair showed she wasn't the young woman she was, she moved quickly and easily around the desk, continuing to berate James as she did.

"Did you know my uncle?" James asked as the woman caught her breath.

The woman froze, before her lip trembled. She reached out for a moment, as if to touch him, but pulled away. "I-I'm terribly sorry," she sniffed and her eyes began to water. "I didn't realise his family had arrived." She stepped around

James and headed quickly for the exit. She staggered slightly and her shoulders began to shake. Rushing over to her, James quickly took her by the shoulders and turned her around, pulling her into a hug.

"My uncle must have been someone special to you, huh?"

She shuddered for a moment, before sighing and taking a step back. Her eyes were still red, but she held herself proudly as she looked James in the eye. "He was my friend. And… Now he's gone."

James smiled sadly at her. "The funeral is the day after tomorrow. I'm getting Baal to let everyone know if they want to come."

She blinked and a few more tears rolled down her cheeks. "You're his heir, aren't you? The one named after him?"

"I am, yes."

She leaned forward and pecked his lips lightly, before straightening. "Thank you. I'll see you at the funeral."

This time he watched as she left without looking like she was about to fall over. As she vanished, Baal appeared, coming inside.

"Do you live here or something?" James asked with a grin.

"Yup," Baal smiled back.

James frowned, then shrugged, "Fair enough. Where am I staying tonight?"

"Your uncle's private suite," Baal gestured for him to follow.

It was part of the main office, at the rear. James had never been in here before, always staying in one of the cabins at the rear of the spa, with his parents. Or in a single room when he was older. Baal left him at the door with a key and James let himself in. It was spacious, and had obviously been cleaned. Whoever the cleaner was had left a card on the key table beside the door to say so. It also had a few watermarks on it, like they'd been crying when they wrote it. So James felt better about his decision to invite all the staff.

Taking a lap of the suite, it was like any other apartment, though much larger than the one James used to live in. The kitchen was large and up to date. There was even a separate lounge and dining. The bathroom had a shower and a spa, and the toilet was in a room by itself. There was a single guest room and the master. Which was almost the same size as the lounge. It was dominated by a large, comfortable looking bed in the centre of the room. Which was just perfect. So after taking another quick shower, James crawled into the large bed and closed his eyes.

The following day was a blur. James got up early. And after passing instructions to Baal to ring anyone who may be interested in attending, he got to work. The morning started with a mower. James was just happy it was a ride-on. The spa was open plan in some places and having to push a mower the whole time would have been exhausting. Starting at the front gate, he tidied up all the grass at the front of the spa and made his way back. Before noon, his father joined him. Appearing shirtless with a hedge trimmer, he got to work on the bushes. James wondered about the shirtless thing, until he spotted his mother watching from inside. They worked long and hard through the day. Carla brought them drinks regularly and they only stopped once for a lunch that was delivered to the ring road so they wouldn't trek anything inside.

Needless to say, when the sun finally dropped below the trees, the father and son duo were tired, sore but very pleased with their results. After enjoying another quiet meal after a hot shower, James made his way back to his suite. Opening the door, he heard the soft music and smelled the scent of roses. Blinking, he looked around, seeing a foldout massage table in the middle of the lounge.

"Hello?" James called.

"Oh!" a voice called back. The bedroom door swung open and the woman from the day before strode out. She was wearing a similar tight outfit as yesterday, just without the cardigan. "Oh good, I was worried you weren't coming."

James smiled, still a little confused, "Well I'm here and… Not to be rude, but…"

"Baal asked me to come in," she smiled, now looking nervous herself. "I am… Was… I worked with your uncle," she paused for a couple breaths. "I'm Mary, I was the one who had to leave quickly yesterday. Baal let me know you were the one who looked after Ms Brown and he let me know you gave her a refund. So when he said you were doing ground works, I remembered James always got so-"

"Mary," James cut her off. She'd started talking so quickly he was losing track. "I won't say no to a massage after today. But you need to relax," he smiled at the flustered older woman. "Now, how's the hand?"

Mary smiled, "It seems fine. I caught it in the door yesterday and couldn't bend it. The doctor said it was swollen and wanted to leave it until today for an x-ray. When I went in today, it felt fine, so… Here I am!"

James nodded, "Alright well… I showered before dinner, have you eaten?"

Her face dropped for a moment, "Ummm…"

"Wanna order a pizza, I promise I won't complain about you getting pizza grease on me," he grinned.

Mary giggled, before blinking back a tear. "I'm sorry. Your uncle used to make jokes like that. I miss him."

James sighed and stepped up to her, giving her a quick hug. Only this time, the scent of her skin and warmth of her body, gave him something else to think about. Clearing his throat and fixing his shirt, James grinned to hide the half chub in his pants. "Right, what kind of pizza do you want?"

Mary smiled and wiped her eyes, "Meatlovers."

James grinned and pulled out his phone, "That one's too easy."

Mary made a very unladylike snort before the two of them burst into laughter. When they both came down, their eyes met and they both had a second fit. James managed to dial the number he needed and place an order. With the Pizza on its way, they headed for the lounge. Mary took a seat on the couch and tucked her legs up. James went and checked the small fridge. Inside was bottled water, various jars of things, some beer and a bottle of wine. Plucking it out, he checked the label.

"I'd love one," Mary called.

With a shrug, James searched the cupboards until he found a bottle opener and some glasses. Then, started pouring. His knowledge of wine went 'red or white' and this was definitely red. He knew the right amount to pour at least and brought a glass to Mary, who took it with a smile.

"I love this brand," she smiled, "Your uncle and I used to have a glass each after a long day."

James nodded, quickly realising how close their friendship must have been. Right now, however, wasn't the time to discuss it. "So how long have you worked here?"

Mary took a sip and leaned back on the couch. "I started here a few years ago. After you left the last time," she smiled sadly. "I came in for an interview. He wanted me to massage him, to make sure I had what it took. Then he made me laugh."

James took a sip of his wine. It was a bit dry, but tasted good as far as he was concerned. "You loved him, didn't you?"

Mary sniffed and took a sip of her wine. "Your uncle was

a difficult man to love," she smiled sadly. "The truth was, he loved everyone and was loved in return. But…"

James's phone dinged, stalling their conversation. Pulling it out, he read the message from the pizza guy out front. So with a smile Mary returned sadly, James darted out to collect it. When he came back in, Mary was washing her hands in the kitchen. She shot him a smile and took her seat on the couch beside her empty wine glass.

"Refill?" James asked, handing her the pizza.

"Please!" She picked up the glass and offered it to him.

James took it with a smile and refilled it. Returning it moments later, as she patted the seat beside her.

"Ummm…"

"How are you going to help me eat this from over there?" She gestured to where James had been sitting. When she saw the look on his face, she pouted, "Really now, do you think I'd eat this whole thing myself?"

James grinned and grabbed his own wine glass, before coming back. "Alright, I'll help. But no promises. I've already eaten."

Mary just grinned, "Well maybe I'll help you work some of it off later." James froze for a moment, as Mary blushed furiously. "I'm sorry… You're just… So much like him."

"It's fine," James replied, plucking the nearest slice and taking a bite. "I'm named after the man after all."

Mary picked up another piece, "He was a good man to be named after."

James smirked and nodded. Then he had a thought. "You gonna hang around, now he's gone?"

Mary paused, "Maybe." She chewed another mouthful and washed it down with a sip of wine. "We'll have to see. But I won't be making any decisions soon. You'll need me for a while anyway."

"Thank you," James smiled.

She shrugged and put down the half eaten piece, before twirling her long silver hair into a bun and slipped a hair tie into place. "Right, get undressed and on the table. I'll wash my hands."

James grinned as he stood, "You just wanna see me with my shirt off."

He'd made it to the table and had the first few buttons undone when he heard Mary's reply. "Duh."

Checking over his shoulder, he couldn't see her. He heard the tap in the kitchen go, so James quickly stripped and got on the table. He hadn't thought the table in the room where he met Ms Brown was all that great, but this portable one seemed in better shape. Shifting around, James relaxed. A moment later, the water cut off and he heard footsteps coming. A set of manicured toes appeared in his vision. Purple nail polish and a toe ring. James grinned, thinking it was cute.

"Now, I've only got the rose scented oil here, are you fine with that?"

"Not fussed," James shrugged as best he could while laying down.

"Great!"

He heard the bottle pop open before feeling the warm liquid on his back. James barely got to take a deep breath, when her hands met his skin. She worked him like a pro and James was left feeling limp as she massaged the ache from his bones. She moved up and rubbed his shoulders, easing the tense feeling he had. Then she moved down his spine and he groaned, feeling a small crack half way down. The ribs were a bit sensitive, but her touch was perfectly between rough enough not to tickle, but soft enough not to bruise. She worked his ass for a bit, making him blush, before working down each leg. By the time she was done, James was drooling. He even let out a small moan as she ran her hands up his body back to his shoulders.

But at that point, as James stared down at her toes, he could see her bare legs. They were smooth, toned and she wore an anklet on the side that lacked the ring. Moving to sit up, he felt her hand press his face back into the mould.

"Relax James. There's no need to get up. But you do need to roll over."

With a sigh, James did as he was told. He paused half way as he realised he had a rather firm problem. "Ummm, Mary, can I have a towel please?"

She giggled despite herself, "I'll take that as a compliment."

James blushed, but felt a towel drape over his ass. Knowing there was no way out of this, he rolled over and concentrated on the ceiling. Mary leaned over him, and James sighed. He was equally relieved and disappointed she was wearing a shirt. He didn't dare turn his head to see if she was in fact not wearing pants.

Leaning over him, she followed the same practice from earlier. Rubbing him from top to bottom. Starting at the shoulders, she leaned over him, dangling her breasts over his face. It was immediately obvious that she wasn't wearing a bra as they swung inside her shirt. James closed his eyes and tried to think about cricket, even as the towel covering his legs began to rise. Mary didn't say a word as she moved down his body. Her hands were heavenly over his chest and abs. She used the same technique that he had the day before, to expose a single leg at a time. She massaged him quickly and efficiently, leaving his legs feeling like jelly.

But he still yelped in surprise as she quickly pulled the towel from his lower half, up so It just obscured his vision.

"Mary!" James groaned, moving to sit up. But froze as her hand pressed into his chest.

"Sir, if you get off the table. I will be forced to leave. Please remain still." James did as he was told and froze. Barely breathing as he heard Mary shuffling around him. "This looks rather sore," she said softly. "It's a good thing you're cooperative, otherwise I might have missed it."

James groaned, he was so hard it almost hurt. But he still needed to say the words, "You don't have to do this."

"Sir, please, I'm a professional."

James gasped as a warm hand gripped the base of his cock. It lightly stroked up, almost to the tip, then back down. She angled his cock towards his chest, before he felt her breath on the head. Silently begging her to suck him, James groaned feeling her hot breath moving lower. The first touch of her lips was at the midpoint, just above her hand. The second a moment later on his balls. As her tongue gently lapped at his balls, James's body twitched. The pressure was firm and her tongue was hot. The feel of her breath told him she was excited about what she was doing. And she was oh so very gentle. James loved it. He'd had his balls sucked before and found it uncomfortable and slightly painful, but this firm lapping of her tongue was heavenly.

She upped the ante after a minute or so. Gently stroking his cock, up and down. Not enough to get him off, but enough to make him extremely uncomfortable. James bit his lip and thought about begging. The tongue on his balls vanished for a moment, as her grip shifted. She held his cock like a phone, cradled in her palm. Her technique shifted as well. Licking from his balls, up the base of his shaft. When she got to the head, her hot breath poured out, warming his glans, before she lifted away and started back at the bottom. Her other hand gently pressed James's legs apart, before cupping his balls in a similar way to his cock. After one final, firmer lick from his balls, to the very tip of his cock, James felt her breath as she hovered over the head of his cock.

"If I suck this, will you fill my pretty little mouth?" Mary asked.

"I hope not," James groaned.

"Oh?" Mary said, kissing his frenulum. "Trying to hold out on me?"

As James opened his mouth to reply, he felt her lips on the head of his cock. In one small movement, they parted and James felt them roll down his cock. Her tongue cradled the underside of his cock as she lowered her head. James waited for her to stop, but she simply didn't. Slowly, her head lowered further and further, taking more of his cock in. Even as she removed her hand, James grit his teeth as she lowered herself further. And as her nose finally nestled amongst his pubic hair, did she finally stop. James felt her hand on his balls begin to massage and lightly pull. Then she swallowed, allowing his cock to enter her throat entirely. Pressing her nose completely into his crotch, she swallowed twice more as James tried desperately not to cum. Pinching her lips closed over his cock, she slowly drew up until her mouth 'popped' off the end.

"Holy shit," James groaned.

Mary giggled, "Well done."

"How… God, I've never…" James sighed.

"You've been such a good boy for me," Mary said, letting him hear the smile on her face. "I'll let you cum down my throat another day if you're good. For now, I'd like to taste it."

James gasped as her mouth closed over his cock. She propped herself up with one hand, while the other kept massaging his balls. Her mouth sucked firmly on the head of his cock like a straw. Her tongue swirled slowly around the base of the head. Concentrated all on the underside of the glans and James felt his balls begin to clench.

"Oh shit!" James grunted.

As the first rope of his seed fired into her mouth. Mary groaned in delight. She kept pace, sucking on the head of his cock, even as he filled her mouth. She loved the taste and wanted as much as she could get. She swirled her tongue over the head, collecting the sticky fluid, while she lengthened the stroking to his balls. She knew he was going to be too dazed to care about a show, so she swallowed, even while continuing to suck. It was a minute later, when she popped her lips off and looked up at his still covered face.

"Does this thing ever go down?"

James chuckled softly. "Would you like to find out?"

She sat up and James wondered if he'd pushed too far. He felt something soft and made of fabric land on his chest. Then the towel was yanked free. Blinking, he grabbed the fabric and lifted it, seeing it was her top from earlier. A soft giggle caught his attention and James rolled onto his side and froze. She was standing in the hall, completely naked, with her hip cocked to one side. Her hand fiddled with her hair as she let it all out to flow down her shoulders.

"You just gonna stare?" she asked, before continuing down to the bedroom.

James almost fell off the table in his eagerness to follow after her. She didn't see him, but she must have heard his mad dash, because her laughter met his ears as he straightened up. Stalking into the room, she was sitting, wide legged at the foot of the bed. Her smoothly shaved pussy pouted slightly. Her labia peeked out and there was a thin line of clear gruel that connected her soft flesh to the floor below.

"Come on now, I'm an old woman," she smiled. "I've done enough waiting, and I'm eager to see you back up those words."

James swallowed, feeling his cock as ready as it ever was, "Better get this started then."

With his cock standing straight out in front, Mary's eyes

watched it hungrily as he came towards her. Bending, he gripped her knees and lifted. Mary squealed in delight, but James ignored her as she fell flat on her back. With her legs up, she laid them on his chest and grinned up at him.

"Well hello there," she smiled. "Have you got something for me?"

James grinned and kissed the side of her ankle. He felt the twitch in her leg at the contact and followed it up with a small bite. "Next time, I want you to wear heels. Red maybe?"

"Next time?" She gasped as his mouth kissed down the inside of her leg. "What makes you think there's going to be a next time?"

Nuzzling into her thigh, mid way between her knee and her crotch, there seemed a sensitive spot that he capitalised on. Her breathing quivered as he nibbled gently. Shifting his body so her knee folded to lay her calf down his back, James pressed her legs wide open, pinning the opposite leg to the mattress. With a final nibble, he kissed his way even lower.

"Tell you what," he said, kissing the sensitive skin in the joint where her leg met her groin. "Next time, I'll do your other leg."

"Oh that's cruel," Mary whined.

But her complaint ended as James lapped at her folds. Very gently, he tasted her and found her delicious. Different from Maggie, but no less divine. Pressing his face a little deeper, James ran his tongue through her labia. He licked her from opening to clit several times until Mary rocked her hips up to meet him. Swallowing her down, James lifted away.

"I know you enjoyed being in charge while you sucked me," he started. "But I get the feeling you don't necessarily like being on top."

As his tongue traced her clit Mary bit the inside of her lip and tried not to moan. "Behind," she gasped. "I love it when I get taken from behind. Pin me down, slap my ass and make me take you."

James gently mouthed her clit for a few moments, before pulling away, grinning at her pained moan. He knew she was close, but after hearing her say that, he had a better idea of what she wanted. Sitting up, he threw off her leg. Her shocked expression was the last thing he saw as he forcefully rolled her over. Dumping her on her front, he gave her ass a hard slap, making Mary yelp and crawl forward. Which was perfect. Diving on top of her, he pinned her down, before sitting back up, dragging her hips towards him.

"James!" she squealed as he speared his cock into her.

Thrusting firmly into her from behind, James spent a few moments holding still, while rocking her hips back and forth into him. Making her fuck him, even as she trembled and gasped. Taking a firmer hold on her ass, James gave her a quick slap, before taking over himself. His sound of his crotch meeting her ass filled the air. Mary's moans got louder and louder. She tried to lift herself up, but James shoved her face back into the mattress. It must have been the right thing to do, as she started forcing herself back into him with each thrust.

"Now now," James grunted.

With his other hand, he palmed her ass, letting his thumb rub against her asshole. She froze and began to tremble.

"Oh fuck!" She cried into the mattress.

Her tunnel clenched down as she came hard. But James didn't stop. He'd heard what she said. To 'make her.' And just because she was having an orgasm, didn't mean he was going to stop making her.

"JaAAAaaaames!" She cried as her legs began to slide out from under her.

True to her words, even this wasn't enough to stop him. Grabbing her firmly around the stomach he held her as she went flat on the bed. James kept thrusting. He was getting close, and Mary was still making all the right noises. Wrapping his arm under her chin, she turned her head and used it as a pillow. It also let him kiss, then bite the side of her neck as he thrust into her from behind.

"Don't," she grunted. "Don't leave a mark, please?"

James heard the tone in her voice and lifted his mouth away. "Whatever you want."

"Kiss me, then fill me up," she gasped as her eyes seemed to focus on nothing.

Leaning over her, James kissed her firmly. She kissed back twice as hard, pressing her tongue into his mouth, as cum surged up to fill her. Shuddering, James hilted himself as deeply as he could inside her and fired ropes of his seed inside her. Mary, moaned as she took a white knuckle grip on the sheets. Her body shuddered through one final orgasm, even as she tried to rock her hips back to take more of him.

As his orgasm subsided, he squeezed his arms around her, holding her in place. She huffed and sighed, while James panted.

"How the fuck are you still hard?" She grumbled.

James laughed softly and she joined him. "Honestly," he chuckled, "I have no idea. But I'm willing to try anything you are."

Mary groaned. "I'd love to, but… I really should be going."

James frowned for a moment, "Oh." Lifting himself off her, he groaned as she sighed, when he pulled his still hard cock out of her.

Mary rolled, before seeing the expression on his face. "What's wrong?"

James shot her a smile. "Being silly, I suppose."

"How so?"

He shrugged. "It's cool. I just figured it was kinda late…" he trailed off.

"James, are you asking me to spend the night?"

"Ummm," He frowned, seeing a shift in her expression. "You're a grown woman, Mary. You don't have to change your plans just for little old me."

She snorted and laughed softly, before shuddering as she let out a sob. James was on her in an instant. Pulling her into his arms, even as she desperately clung to him for a few moments.

"Hey, are you sure you're okay getting home? It's fine if you wanna stay here. If you're not comfortable we me in the bed, there's plenty of other-"

Mary kissed him. She kissed him hard and kept kissing him until he moaned and lost track of what he was saying. Only as she pulled away, he was faced with a beautiful older woman, beaming at him as tears rolled down her cheeks.

"I hope you're not offended by this James. But you're just like him, only… It's like you're the best of him, but with your own twist that makes you so much more."

James smiled, slightly confused, but shrugged. "I guess we have our similarities. He was a good guy."

She smiled back, "He was. And so are you, and… Yes, I'd love to spend the night."

"He used to send you home, didn't he?" James asked.

Mary frowned, then nodded. "If we drank, he organised me a room, but… No, I never spent the night."

James offered his hand. When she took it, he helped her up, before pulling the blanket down and laying her gently on the mattress. Hitting the light, he crawled into the bed beside her and pulled the blanket back up over both of them. Mary pressed herself into his side in the dark and raised her leg over his own, giggling as it brushed his still hard cock.

"You know," she said softly. "If you're still hard."

Shoving her over onto her back, Mary's legs came up to cradle his sides as he slid his cock into her drooling pussy.

"Kiss me, please?" She begged.

James closed his eyes as he kissed her softly, and ground his cock into her depths, making her gasp and tremble. He held her close as he slowly made love to her. And Mary decided he was getting his dick sucked for breakfast.

CHAPTER THREE

aal was positively beaming when James turned around. He'd just said goodbye to Mary, who was going home to change for the funeral. James was feeling slightly bow legged from the blowjob she gave him moments after her alarm started blaring… And the subsequent blow job he got in the shower, after bending her over the bathroom sink and taking her from behind. Either way, he was feeling pretty good about himself, even if his dick seemed to be doing more talking than usual.

"Morning Baal," James nodded.

"Morning James," Baal smiled. "Enjoy your evening?"

James swallowed nervously. "Yeah and ummm… Thanks for organising that massage. I feel pretty good today."

"That's not the massage," Baal winked.

James blushed and Baal sighed. "She's right though."

"Hmmm?"

"You're all the best of your uncle, with your own twist."

James looked at the smiling older man and frowned. "Baal, are you spying on me?"

"Not at all James," Baal shook his head. "I have only your best interests in heart, just like I had your uncles. But he wouldn't listen."

"Baal, what happened to my uncle?"

The older man's smile seemed to droop for a moment and he sighed. "Ever heard, be careful what you wish for?"

"Of course," James frowned.

"One day, a man made a wish. That wish was granted, in a sense and things began to happen that spiralled out of control."

"Like what?" James asked.

Baal looked uncomfortable for a moment. "James, I can't answer that, at least not yet."

James frowned. He knew Baal was holding out on him and the situation made him nervous. But something about the older man gave him a sense of ease. "Alright, when?"

"Soon," Baal replied with a modest grin. "Maybe a couple weeks."

James sighed and nodded. "Alright, keep your secrets," he shot a grin at the older man.

Baal shook his head, "That was bad, even I got that one."

James was met in the dining room by his parents and they had a quiet breakfast together. The kitchen was a little livelier today as they prepared for the funeral. The funeral itself was being held in a small chapel in town. The wake would be held here at the spa. James had no idea who was actually going to be there, but Baal had assured him that everything had been sorted. James's parents had already organised the funeral arrangements and all James had to do was attend. So after breakfast James headed back to his room.

He had an hour before they had to leave and took another shower. It was the first time he'd had one since he got here, where he didn't share it with a woman. And he found it strangely odd, like that was wrong for some reason. Nobody owed him their time, so James shook off the strange feeling and scrubbed himself down. When he came out of the room, a suit had been laid on the bed, ready and waiting. James frowned, not knowing who had put it there, but figured it was his mother or maybe Baal.

Twenty minutes later, James was standing in the reception, looking around the room. It really hadn't changed since he was a kid. The carpet was worn, the paint had faded and the atmosphere had lost the lustre he remembered from his youth. That wasn't to say anything was in disrepair. It just badly needed an update.

"Thoughts?" Baal said, walking up behind him.

James shrugged, "Needs paint, carpet, maybe a good clean."

Baal nodded, "You'll need to reopen soon if you want that."

James nodded, "I'll need to reopen soon if I want to reopen at all. I just hope James has enough old clients that they'll trickle back for nostalgia if nothing else."

Baal nodded, "Give it a couple weeks to settle in and we'll reevaluate the situation."

James frowned at the mention of the time frame again, but nodded. "Right. Well… Are you coming?"

"Of course," Baal smiled a little sadly this time. "A chance to say goodbye to an old friend."

James nodded as the sound of footsteps approached from behind. James turned and saw both his parents dressed for the funeral. "You ready?"

They both nodded and stepped past. It must have been pre-arranged as James and Baal both climbed into the back of his parents SUV as they made their way into town. It had been a little while since he had been here. It hadn't changed all that much. The corner shop where he'd bought drinks was under a new franchise. Old Mr. Crochet was still at the counter reading a paper. They drove through town and pulled up at the chapel. People were already milling about waiting for the doors to open as James stepped out.

The crowd seemed to move with their arrival. Some of the younger people came up to Baal and spoke softly with the older man. James guessed these were staff and by the number of them. They all seemed a bit sad, but happy to be included and James hoped they would all stay on. Hiring for a massage parlour in this town would not be easy. Most of the people who worked at the spa grew up with the idea of working there. A few others were hired in from outside town, but they were hit and miss. Sometimes they came from large cities thinking the quiet life might be better, until they realised the internet quality was poor and they couldn't shop on a Sunday. So they left again.

"James," A woman called.

Turning, he smiled as Mary came towards him. She was dressed in a slim black dress and matching heels. "Mary," James smiled and opened his arms for a hug.

The older woman leaned in and hugged him firmly. James returned the gesture, mindful of her leaning away to spare her makeup.

"James, who's this?" His mother asked.

"Mum, dad," James smiled as Mary stood and looked nervous for a moment. "This is Mary, one of Jame's friends who works at the spa."

Mum eyed Mary for a moment, before accepting what James had said and offering her hand to shake. "Carla, this is my husband Matthew."

"It's lovely to meet you both," Mary shook her hand, before accepting the same from Matthew. "I'm sorry for your loss. James was a good friend for a number of years."

Dad looked a little sad, "Thank you."

They drifted into conversation for a while and James just got into the groove of things. Some people he knew, others he did not. Everyone had a kind word once they found out who he was. When the doors to the chapel opened, James was in the front row beside his parents, Baal, Mary and a few others. The funeral director made his speech. It was rather short, and spoke of love and loss in equal measure. It was fitting for a man who wouldn't want anyone to mourn his loss. No if James were here, he'd be wanting them to celebrate the good times.

The funeral continued, with James and his father leading the pallbearers. They carried the coffin to the hearse and followed behind to the other side of town. He was buried in a shady spot, between two large cedars. And as the last people said goodbye, James was left alone.

"Well James," he started. "I don't know why you picked me… I mean other than the name. Nothing actually has to change I guess." James let out a loud sigh. "I'm gonna try and make you proud. I'll get the spa back into shape, keep it going and one day, I'll pass it on like you did."

James felt the wind brush past and a feather of weight pressed on his shoulder. He knew it was nothing, but it somehow felt right. With a final sigh, James turned and headed back towards his parents who were waiting by the car.

"You okay?" his father asked.

James nodded, "Yeah. Let's get back, I'm hungry."

Matthew laughed, then threw the cemetery a sad smile, and got in the driver's seat. The drive back was quiet, and James had time to reflect. He really did want to pick up the spa. It was in the family for decades since James had started it fresh out of college. He'd built it up bit by bit from a single cabin, to the small resort complex it is today. When they pulled up, James headed for his suite, wanting to get into something more comfortable. He froze, seeing Mary leaning against the door.

"Mary?"

"I needed somewhere to change," she smiled and held up an evening bag.

"Oh," James smiled. "Come on in then."

Mary stepped back and allowed James to unlock the door. Before James moved aside and gestured for her to enter first. "Such a gentleman," she giggled.

Once inside, she made her way into the bathroom, while James headed for the bedroom and changed out of his suit. Getting into a comfortable pair of jeans and a t-shirt, James stepped out of the room and froze. Mary was fixing her heels. A bright red pair that gave her legs a nice shape. They paired well with the outfit she wore. It was conservative as it was sexy and she smiled as she saw him staring.

"Come on, you need introductions."

James nodded, before stepping closer. Mary led him out of the suite and into the dining room. It had been opened up with a dance floor in the centre of the room. The kitchens were loud and there were numerous people in the room. Mary led him to each group and gave introductions. Those he had met at the funeral smiled and greeted him like an old friend. Others he hadn't had the chance to meet yet, expressed more condolences.

As they made their way around the room, Baal was sitting with James's parents. While they smiled sadly, they also laughed and James left them to it. A short while later food was brought out and James was introduced to the cooks. He remembered them fondly from when he was younger. Laura, the head even went as far as giving his cheek a pinch like she had when he was young. With the food in place, drinks began to flow and someone put music on. James found himself holding Mary in his arms while they slowly danced around the floor. He spotted his mother's disapproving frown a few times, but he stuck out his tongue at her. After that, she got the hint and went back to ignoring him.

The evening wrapped up early, as the spa was going to be open in the morning. Everyone James had spoken to were keen to return to their old positions and he had spoken to Baal about starting up the booking process. There was no reason to keep things slow and the business needed to make money, or they'd have to let people go. Something James didn't want to do.

"James honey?"

James released Mary and turned to his mother, who gestured for him to follow. Shooting an apologetic glance at Mary, who waved him off, James went with his mother. She led him out to reception where his father was waiting.

"Son," he started. "That woman, Mary."

James groaned, "Please don't do this."

"She's as old as I am!" His mother remarked.

"Mum," James sighed. "Look, I'm a grown man, I make my own decisions now."

"But she's so much older!" Mum complained again.

"So what? Vaginas have an expiration date?"

His mother flinched and took a step back, "No... Your father and I-"

"Do we really need to have this conversation?" James motioned at plugging his ears.

That at least broke some tension and they had a small laugh.

His father cleared his throat, "Son, we're just worried about where it's heading. You've only known her for what, a day?"

James groaned and rubbed his eyes as he turned away. "Look, she was one of Uncle James's friends and she works here. She came over yesterday to give me a massage, we had dinner and yes, she spent the night. We're not talking monogamy, we're not talking about marriage, we're not talking about kids. We went at it like rabbits and cuddled a bit. Now can you drop it?"

"Son-"

"Carla, he's not a child any more. I told you talking about it was a mistake."

Carla swatted her husband on the arm and turned back to James. "Son, we just want what's best for you."

"Right," James nodded. "And the moment I find a woman to mother my children, I'll make some introductions. In the meantime, can you just accept a beautiful woman wants to have sex with me, without getting weird about her age?"

"But-"

"Carla!" His father tugged her arm.

"Matthew-"

"Carla please… They're not doing anything wrong, let's leave it."

"She's just so-"

"Smart, attractive, good with her hands, great in-"

"SON!"

"MUM!"

James held his mothers gaze while she grumbled at him. "Fine," she sighed.

Turning on the spot, she stormed out and towards where they'd parked. Matthew watched her go for a moment, before stepping closer and nudging him with his elbow. He gave James a wide grin and winked.

"Oh god dad, take her home would you?"

"Gladly," his father smirked. "When she gets in these moods, she's feisty."

"DAD!"

His father just laughed as he stepped through the front doors and towards his wife, who was standing cross armed by the car. James watched them both get in, before turning and heading back into the dining room. There, he found Mary nursing a bottle of water.

"You okay?" James asked, taking a seat.

She smiled a little sadly and nodded her head. "Yeah, just waiting for the inevitable."

"Inevitable?"

Mary turned and fixed James with a look, "Isn't this the part, where you tell me your mother disapproves of you spending time with an older woman?"

James shrugged, "No, I figured this was time to drag you back to my room, rip those clothes off you and make sure I even up those legs of yours."

They burst into James's room a minute later, giggling. James took Mary in his arms and kissed her as he walked her backward towards the room.

"No," she murmured. "Wait." James pulled away, only for her to peck his lips one final time. Then she slipped past and darted into the bathroom. "Be naked and with wine!"

James grinned and went to the fridge. He grabbed the wine they'd started the night before and a pair of glasses, before heading back to the room. He set the bottle on the nightstand and poured two glasses with what was left. Sitting down on the bed, James removed his shoes, before yanking off his shirt. Standing, he undid the button for his jeans, when he heard a noise.

Turning, Mary smiled nervously as she bit her lip. "Do you like?"

James eyed her for a moment. She wore a transparent babydoll. It was powder blue and did absolutely nothing for her modesty. She shifted, causing it to sway against her hips.

Those hips had tiny strings attached and James swallowed at the sight of the matching panties.

"Ummm," James groaned.

Mary giggled softly, before turning around. Bending, James's mouth went dry. Not only were the panties crotchless, but he could see the silver ring from a buttplug she was wearing.

"How about this angle?"

She didn't even hear his approach until his hands were on her. Mary let out a small squeal as one hand wrapped around her waist. The other James used to steer his cock into her. She was already wet and ready for him. Mary just hadn't been expecting him to be so forceful. James on the other hand felt a primal need to have her. Consequences be damned, James pushed his cock into her and found a firm rhythm.

"Oh fuck!" Mary whimpered as her legs quivered in her red heels.

But James held her steady. He leaned against her, pinning her in place, while pulling on her hips to drive himself deeper inside her. He grunted and snarled as he felt her tunnel pulse around his cock. James, feeling restricted by his jeans, paused just long enough to shove them down to his ankles before kicking them aside. Wrapping his arms around Mary, he picked her up and carried her, still impaled on his cock, to a nearby table. Putting her down, James lifted her knee and made her stand on one leg, with her other knee resting on the table. Mary felt his hands in the middle of her back and she leaned onto the table to support herself.

"James?"

"Shh!" he swatted her ass with the palm of his hands. "Quiet while I fuck you."

Pumping his hips, James had a much better angle here. He

could stroke his entire length into Mary's slippery pussy. Mary on the other hand could do little more than hold on. She had loved how he had taken her the night before, but this was something else. She felt like she had when she was younger. She felt sexy, wanted, and she wished desperately that she could have children. Surely any man who could fuck like this was worth spreading his genes.

"Oh god!" Mary cried.

"What did I say?" James demanded.

Reaching around, James cupped her mouth and muffled her cries as she came around his cock. James, remembering what she had said the night before, kept thrusting as she spasmed around him. Gritting his teeth, James wrapped his arms around her and pinned her to his chest as he emptied himself inside her. Mary gasped, feeling the throb of his cock and tried to force herself back. He held her still and she was left panting with need as the combination of their juices leaked down her legs.

"James?" she sighed when he uncovered her mouth. But he still refused to let go of her. "You okay?"

James blinked, even as held Mary in his arms. Loosening his grip, he stepped back, allowing his still hard cock to slide out of her and he watched as his deposit began leaking onto the carpet.

"You're so fucking sexy," James said without thinking.

Mary grinned and sagged slightly in relief. "You're not so bad yourself, y'know?" She turned around and saw his cock still standing to attention. "Does that thing ever go down?"

James blushed and shrugged, "I ummm… Not really."

Mary smiled and lightly stroked the head of his cock with her fingers. "Should I maybe clean this off?"

"Nah," James grinned and took her hand, directing her to the bed. "I'm just going to get it dirty again."

"Oh? You wanna put it in my ass?"

James froze, "I meant I was going to fuck you again, but sure. If you want it in your ass, we can do that too."

Mary's heart rate increased. She wore the buttplug for her own pleasure. She'd only done anal properly a couple of times. But… She turned and saw his hungry glare fixated on her. She blushed, "Yeah, maybe we could try it."

James gave her a small shove and Mary giggled as she fell onto the bed. He loomed over her for a moment, before smiling. "I seem to remember I have a leg to even up?"

"Oh," Mary smiled and raised her leg. "Is this how it's going to be? Take advantage of the poor old lady, then make love to her as an apology?"

James took her leg, smiling at the heels. They were quite nice and gave a nice aesthetic. He kissed her ankle and started to work his way down, rubbing his hands and nibbling anywhere that got a reaction.

He stopped at the spot between her knee and crotch he knew made her squirm the night before and smiled. "No, I'd planned on feeding you some of our combined mess, then pinning your knees to your shoulders and seeing if I can make you scream."

Lightly nuzzling into the spot, Mary gasped and writhed. James lightly cupped her sex, smearing their juices onto his fingers, before reaching up and pressing them into Mary's mouth. She moaned as she sucked his fingers clean, so James repeated the process twice more. Satisfied, James rolled Mary onto her side and straddled her leg. Lifting the other, he threw it over his shoulder. Taking his cock, James felt no resistance as he pushed inside Mary's pussy once again.

"Oh fuck!" Mary choked.

"Yes, that's the idea," James grunted, rocking his hips.

Mary, with his weight on one leg and her other trapped over her shoulder, could do nothing as he fucked her. Long deep strokes drove her onward as she gripped the bedsheets in an attempt to ground herself in the moment. James watched as the confident, sure-fire woman was reduced to animalistic grunts and gasps as James set the pace he wanted. Reaching down between them, James gently stroked her clit, making Mary shudder and cry out.

"That's a good girl," James grinned. "You cum on that cock. You're allowed."

"Th-thank you!" Mary squealed as her body began to spasm.

But James didn't care. The harder she came, the better as far as he was concerned. Until she genuinely wanted him to stop, he was going to keep doing what he wanted. Mary for that matter, was having some serious doubts about James's humanity. She'd been with men before who had a bit of stamina. But this was otherworldly. He'd already filled her once, and was still fucking her as he had before. She could still taste the results he'd fed her from their time on the table. Now it was agonising ecstasy. She felt herself peaking for her third orgasm, that no doubt would be even stronger than the one before. When she felt the plug in her ass move.

James slipped his finger into the ring of her buttplug. Mary's eyes were crossing again and he knew she was about to cum. Giving the plug a small pull, he watched her ass stretch as the plug started to come free. He let it slip back inside and Mary shuddered and cried out as she gripped the sheets.

"Are you going to cum again?" James asked, repeating the slow tug on her buttplug.

"Yes!" Mary cried out, almost sounding like she was in pain. "God yes!"

"Good," James grinned. "When you start to cum, I'm going to pull this out," Jame wiggled the plug once again.

"Please!" Mary whimpered. "Please fuck my ass!"

"Needy little slut, aren't you?" James laughed as he increased his pace, enjoying the slick feeling of her pussy slipping over his cock. "I didn't even have to ask."

"Keep making me cum," Mary begged. "I don't care how!"

She shuddered and gasped. James felt her pussy contract and he wiggled her buttplug harder than he had earlier. Mary's scream let out, as the silver plug came free in his hand. Pulling his cock free, James mopped up some of their juices with his fingers, before sliding them deep into Mary's relaxed ass. Immediately Mary gasped and bit down on the sheets at the anal intrusion. But it was nothing compared to the feeling as his cock slid into her.

"More!" She begged.

James stared down at half his cock inside her and grinned. "You want the whole thing?"

"Please?"

James grinned and slowly pushed his entire length into her ass. Mary just shuddered as her next orgasm hit out of nowhere. She'd had a few orgasms over the years from anal play, but this was the first time she had cum with a cock in her ass. James let her enjoy it, gently rocking his hips back and forth as she spasmed around him. As she came down, James shifted them to one side, releasing her trapped leg. Then, he rolled Mary flat, and lifted her other leg over his shoulder. Then he leaned down, folding Mary in half. She was dazed and half out of her mind. But when he kissed her, she frantically kissed back. Holding her in place, James took his time, sliding his cock in and out of her ass. He figured if this happened again, he'd be able to take her hard like she wanted. For now, James made simple love to her her ass, while she trembled and came around him.

His orgasm rose up as he felt warm fluid pooling between their crotches. And James hilted himself in her ass and started to fill her up. Mary, feeling the pulse of his cock shuddered through one last orgasm of her own. Slipping her legs down from his shoulders, James kissed Mary gently as she stared up at him.

"Are you going to fuck my ass again?" She asked

James's cock gave a small throb at the thought, but he smiled down at her. "How about we take a shower. See how we feel when we get back to bed?"

"Am I staying the night?"

James kissed her firmly for several moments, before pulling away. "I'd love for you to stay."

She smiled back up at him. "You need to…"

"Oh right," James laughed.

Sitting up, he watched as his cock slid free of Mary's ass. There was little mess, not that James cared. They were heading for the shower. Lifting her legs, he undid her heels, earning a grateful smile, before helping her stand.

"Thank you," she blushed.

By the time they were back in bed, Mary was feeling a little sore. When James had tried to apologise, she'd kissed him quiet. Before admitting she wanted him to fuck her harder next time. That had made him blush like an idiot as he pulled her close.

James woke at sunrise after they had forgotten to close the blinds. But Mary stirred as well. That led to a morning of long, slow sex that had them both up and ready well before their alarms were supposed to go off. Mary's overnight bag contained her work uniform and for the first time since he had kissed someone goodbye from reception, she didn't actually leave. Instead, she made a vague promise about visiting his office one day and went to take care of their latest VIP. James on the other hand, spent his day on the phone, booking and rebooking clients. He and Baal sat together and went over the budget. The spa was only barely breaking even with the VIP clients that had come in. There was a little company savings to go around and give them breathing room. However, the business was essentially one major expense from closing down.

So that became the new priority. Getting clients. James worked hard, giving discounts to anyone who had been affected by the funeral. Most had been gracious when James explained the situation and were happy to rebook. A few others were less so and James offered them refunds instead. Baal had originally questioned his decision, but accepted when James had explained that he would prefer not to do business with people who couldn't empathise with a family death, they weren't worth keeping as clients.

At the end of the day, when James was feeling sore from being seated for most of it. He staggered into his suite, to the sight of Mary wearing nothing but an apron, as she cooked him a steak dinner.

"Mary?"

"Don't get used to this buster!" She called back. "I have plants to water, so you're on your own tomorrow. I'm not some live in girlfriend to have hanging around-"

James grabbed her and pulled her away from the stove, before kissing her firmly. She blushed as she pulled away, but turned her scowl back on him.

"As I was saying-"

"Thank you Mary," James cut her off.

Mary frowned, and turned back to the stove, flipping his steak. "You're lucky you're cute, mister."

"Extremely lucky. I have a beautiful woman cooking me dinner. I didn't expect it, but I'm very thankful."

"Good," Mary called as James moved towards the shower. "Because after you're fed, I want you dick inside me so when Miss Cinch does her caring elderly neighbour trick, I feel you running down my legs."

James paused, "Miss Cinch?"

"She's been at me for years about getting a husband," Mary called. "Now hurry up and get ready. I want to be pinned to your bed with your dick inside me, within the hour!"

James grinned and yanked off his shirt, "Yes ma'am!"

4

CHAPTER FOUR

James woke up and smiled at the sight before him. Mary's form, illuminated in the early morning sunlight. James didn't care about her age, she was warm, soft and lovely in all the ways it mattered. Waking up next to her was just a bonus that seemed to happen with more frequency over the last month. After that first couple of nights, she spent some time away. Sure they caught up over lunch, chatted like friends and spent the occasional lunch break in a storeroom naked from the waist down.

By the end of the second week, work had picked up, and those midday romps were getting difficult to accommodate for both of them. So she supplemented it with evening romps that sometimes led to overnight stays. Then, over the last week, her sex drive had ramped up somewhat. They'd made jokes and James had brought up the possibility of pregnancy, and then held her as she teared up while explaining ovarian cancer in her mid twenties. The fact remained, James found himself entertaining more often than not, and she was ravenous.

"You're watching me," Mary grumbled softly.

James smiled and shifted his arm to pull her closer. She smiled and nuzzled into his shoulder. "Sorry, does it bother you?"

"No," she murmured into his neck as she lifted her chin and kissed along his collar bone. "But you should make it up to me anyway."

James grinned as he felt Mary's hand gently stroke his morning glory.

Still with a stupid grin on his face, James stepped into his office and took a seat. Going through his emails, there was one that came up, a VIP booking for Ms Margaret Brown. It had been forwarded by Baal who had been taking care of the bookings while James helped out with the business itself. Between yard work, hedge trimming and the occasional massage, they were finally making money again. Not a lot, but enough that James was no longer worried about their long term viability.

Still, the issue of Margaret, or Maggie as she wanted to be called, was going to be complicated. Things had been going smoothly with Mary, and he hadn't thought to bring up the situation. Now he was running the risk of having two very lovely women, very mad at him. Checking the booking, he could see Maggie wasn't supposed to arrive till noon, and it was almost ten. Flicking through Mary's schedule, James could see she had a gap at half past. Nodding, he took out his phone and sent her a text to meet him.

Then it was a simple matter of waiting. James fiddled around online, looking at various companies that could refurbish the spa. Others for the landscaping, seeing as he didn't want to be doing it permanently. A firm knock on the door snapped him back to attention. James glanced at the time and it was a little after half past.

"Come in!" He called

The door swung open and Maggie rushed in, tossing aside a small duffel bag. James had only a moment to prepare, before she literally threw herself over the desk knocking him flat on his back. Before he could react, her tongue was in his mouth and her hands were pulling at his clothes. James kissed back for a few moments, before collecting himself, and grabbed both her hands. She pulled away, suddenly looking very concerned, but didn't get any further as a loud voice growled.

"Just what the hell is this?"

Maggie blushed fiercely, before pecking James's lips once more and standing up. "I ummm. I'm sorry, I'll just-"

"Maggie?" Mary gasped. "Wha-"

"Mary?" Maggie froze in place. "I... Oh..."

Then as one, both their gazes snapped to James as he sat himself up. "You... You know each other then?"

James had never felt so uncomfortable than in this very moment. After getting up and re-tucking his shirt, Mary was glaring at the two of them from the corner of the room. Maggie on the other hand, looked embarrassed, but not entirely upset as she sat demurely in the seat opposite James's desk. Bending, he awkwardly picked up his chair in the dead silence of the room, before retaking his seat.

"Well... I suppose we should talk about this."

"I think so," Mary growled softly.

Maggie flinched slightly, but nodded her head. "Have you two been together long?"

"Since the day after he got here," Mary replied coolly as James refused to speak. He wasn't aware they were 'together.' The conversation had never happened. But he wasn't about to commit verbal suicide be saying that out loud.

"We slept together only once, while I was here on my last booking. I believe that was before you then, so no, he didn't cheat." The slight softening in Mary's glare was a relief for

James. No matter what happened, he didn't want anyone hurt by this. "And, if I'd known, I wouldn't have thrown myself across the table to get at him. I'm sorry."

Mary sighed, "It's fine. You didn't know, it's not like we've spoken much in the last decade."

Maggie flinched slightly, "Yes my... Ex... Made my social life rather difficult." She turned to Mary and shot her a sad smile. "I missed you so much."

James just watched as the two women collapsed on each other. They broke down in tears fractions of a second apart. Maggie barely got up before Mary pulled her into a hug, and James just tried to think of anything other than the two of them naked.

"Please forgive me," Maggie begged softly.

"Of course I do," Mary smiled as they pulled away, but Maggie shook her head.

"For this," she said. Turning, she picked up her bag and took out a white stick.

Mary froze, seeing it, but Maggie simply placed it on the desk before James. James frowned for a moment, before picking it up. It was about the width of his finger, and about fifteen centimeters long. At one end was a cap, and the other was a little window with two faded lines on it. And...

"Maggie?" James asked softly. "This... Isn't possible."

"You had a hysterectomy," Mary frowned. "I drove you to the hospital myself."

Maggie nodded and pulled out a folder. Pulling it open, she withdrew a stack of documents. "These are photos of the ultrasound, showing..." She sniffed and wiped away a tear. "Showing that my womb has somehow grown back into place."

The slam of the door made James jump. Mary's sudden absence was a concern, but not unexpected. For now, James was focussed on Maggie's hands as she placed the paperwork on the desk. When he looked up at her, she was crying softly, but standing firm. James plucked up the first image, clearly showing the ultrasound. There was a whole stack, taken of various positions, showing everything from her cervix to her ovaries. The last page was a statement written up by the doctor stating that for unknown reasons, her womb had grown back. It seemed healthy, functional and on the last page, included a note that pregnancy had been achieved, so further testing was not recommended at this time. Flipping back through each photo, he found one that had a small grey circle he'd missed. Picking up the image, all there was, was a strange, tiny blob.

"Is that?"

"Mhm," Maggie's lip trembled.

"And, you're sure..." James gulped, not wanting to continue that line of questioning.

But Maggie nodded her head. "I've been with two men in the last ten years, and only one has touched me in the last three."

"I... I don't know what to say," James admitted, staring at the image.

The door burst open again and Mary stormed into the room. She had an odd expression on her face.

"Mary?" Maggie quickly moved to see what was wrong.

But Mary was staring at James, trembling. She gave a small hiccup, before her legs wobbled. Maggie grabbed her as she went to the floor and Mary sat bow-legged on the floor.

"Mary honey, what's wrong?" Maggie stroked her hair and gently rocked her, trying to get a response from her old friend.

James just stared at her, before realising, clutched in her hand, was something white. "Mary?"

She blinked up at him as tears rolled down her cheeks. "It's impossible."

"Mary?" Maggie tried again. "Talk to me honey, please, you're scaring me."

"Ovarian cancer," Mary mumbled. "I never told you. Never told anyone."

Breaking eye contact with James, she stared into Maggie's eyes for a moment, before holding up a white stick.

"That… That's one of my tests," Maggie asked, glancing over at her bag.

Mary nodded as she began to tremble. "I'm gonna be a mummy."

Then she imploded. Bursting into tears, she went from beaming happily, to big ugly crying with the drool. James scrambled around the desk and grabbed both women and they clung to him just as tightly. Life was suddenly far more complicated than he could ever imagine.

James finished up with a hot towel to wipe away the excess oil from Mr Harrison's back. Mr Harrison was a little disappointed that it wasn't Mary doing his usual massage, but James had entertained his talks about the war his father fought in. Sure enough, by the end, Mr Harrison had forgotten all about Mary and James left him alone to dress. There was no further business to attend to for him. He spent the day covering Mary's clients. She wasn't in the right headspace to continue working and with Maggie at her side, James had handed over the keys for his suite and left them to it. It was then up to him to simply explain a personal emergency to each of her clients, that he then took on himself. They all seemed understanding and a few were even worried about her, which warmed James's heart.

Now however, the day was over, Mr Harrison was getting dressed and all James had to do was politely show him out. And a few minutes, after doing so, James locked the glass doors and turned, freezing at the sight of Baal beaming in delight.

"Baal," James sighed. "I wish you wouldn't do that."

"Oh," he grinned. "But it's so much fun, and I'm in a celebrating mood."

James nodded, "Well… I think I am too."

"Yes, two pregnancies," Baal nodded.

James smiled, knowing he understood, before freezing. "How did you know?"

"One day, a wise and powerful lord, had a wife who suffered a rather unfortunate accident that left her unable to bear children. Rather than accept the inevitable and choose a second wife, he consulted with his priests for a better solution," Baal smiled thinly. "They bartered with the gods of their time and made a deal to help their lord. But in the lord's eagerness, he overlooked certain aspects."

"Baal?" James asked, but he flashed James a smile with jagged teeth that silenced him immediately.

"The deal was not struck with the wife, but with the lord himself. He was given a gift, allowing him to impregnate any woman he slept with. At first there was much rejoicing. But then the lord's mistresses all fell pregnant as well. And not just mistresses, but women of his courts. Each new pregnancy was a threat to his wife's child, and so he swore never to do it again. But that was not part of the deal." Baal sighed and shook his head. "When the lord stopped creating new life to feed his side of the bargain, he began to waste away. When he came back, looking for answers, he was appalled at what I told him."

"You?" James asked.

Baal smiled again, but with a sad tinge. "Your family is cursed James. A simple curse, one your uncle decided to exploit for a time, but ultimately did not fulfill. You were named heir of this place, because your uncle knew you would take on the burden of responsibility."

"Uncle James, died, because of you?" James asked, emotion colouring his voice.

But Baal shook his head. "No, your uncle died because a wise man, many centuries ago made a rash decision on a deal he did not fully understand. You uncle got the same explanation you're getting, only it was after many months of me trying to help him and failing spectacularly. Your uncle knew what he was doing, and now you do too. I live in this world, on the residual life force left over from the pregnancies you will create."

James threw a punch. His hand whipped around, curling into a fist, but right before impact, his hand was snared in one, grey, with cracked skin and long claws. But James didn't care, "I won't let you hurt them!"

"No!" Baal hissed, returning to normal features. "Weren't you listening? Residual!" He snapped, flicking James between the eyes making him blink and rub his forehead. "Now, where were we?" He scratched his head, "That's right! Babies! Yes, you make babies, I feed off the energy, everybody wins!"

"And if I don't make babies?"

Baal frowned for a moment, "I learned a long time ago, that humans weren't the mindless drones I believed they were. They're clever, insightful, artistic and sometimes truly marvelous beings. Believe it or not, your uncle and I were firm friends and he asked me to look out for you." Baal reached up and patted James's shoulder, "If you don't you will die. A little older than your uncle, but you will die, young, with many, many years before you."

James groaned and nodded his head. "And why didn't uncle want to take you up on this?"

Baal looked uncomfortable for a moment and nodded, "You're the last man in your line. If you stopped right here, you would die, and I would cease to be in this realm. I can't support that decision, but if you choose to do so, I will not stop you either."

"I've got two pregnant ladies-"

"Girls," Baal shook his head. "The curse runs through the men. The deal was with the husband, not the wife."

James blinked and nodded. "Right…"

"Anyway," Baal sighed. "That's pretty much it. If you decide to have lots of babies, you'll live to a ripe old age. There's little bonuses in there as well, for health, luck and so forth. Wouldn't do to have you kick the bucket a few years in because of a heart attack or something. But you will age, and one day you will pass on, same as everyone else, and if you do not have a male heir, I will pass alongside you."

"What's the deal with the statue?"

Baal smirked, "That's the offering made to me all those years ago. It serves as a base for my power, which was that nasty little jab you got."

Nodding, James sighed, "Alright, is there any rules to this? Can I tell people?"

"You can," Baal smiled. "I've told you all the rules. You make babies, you get to live. You don't make babies, we both die." With the same charming smile he had when James met him that first day, Baal turned and started walking back into wherever it was that he actually stayed in this place. "Good luck explaining that to anyone without sounding crazy!"

"What?" James groaned, realising the depth of the situation. "How am I going to explain this to Mary and Maggie?!"

"You'll find a way, I'm sure," Baal smiled, before stepping around the corner and vanishing from view.

"Shit," James swore.

Heading back to his suite, James pushed open the doors. Inside, the lights were dim, soft music was playing and there was both Mary and Maggie in the kitchen. They were fully dressed, but now in comfortable clothing and aprons.

"Ladies," James called, closing the door.

In unison, they both stopped what they were doing and rushed towards him. Maggie was a moment behind, after taking a pot of the heat, so Mary got to him first. Plastering herself to him, she kissed James with enough passion, he was feeling out of breath by the time she pulled away. He was then subjected to an equally passionate kiss from Maggie. Gasping for air as Maggie pulled away he stared at both of them as they beamed in unison.

"Hi," James smiled awkwardly as he tried to reign in his erection.

"We made dinner," Maggie smiled back.

Mary leaned in and pecked James on the lips once more, "Go take a quick shower, we'll get things ready out here."

As they released him, James nodded, still nervous about why they were both acting this way. But he wasn't about to turn down a good thing either. So with a smile, he headed straight for the shower. James frowned at his mutinous erection and quickly got in the shower. After wetting himself James scrubbed himself clean and in record time, got himself dry. With a towel wrapped around his waist, James ignored the wolf whistle, as he made it into the bedroom and got changed into something more comfortable. Coming back out, James could smell wonderful things coming from the kitchen. Mary intercepted with a glass of wine and directed him to the couch to wait.

A moment later, both Mary and Maggie approached with three plates. Mary sat directly beside him, passing over a plate, while Maggie sat on the other side of Mary.

"Thank you, both of you," James smiled as he looked at a pasta dish he didn't recognise.

"Eat up, there's desert after," Mary smiled.

James nodded and tucked in. It was like a carbonara, but with prawns and a little spice. James couldn't help the small moan of appreciation as he tucked in. The ladies beside him smiled at one another, before tucking into their own meals. James barely came up for air until he was finished. With a smile and a loud sigh, he leaned back into the couch and let out a groan.

"That was amazing."

"I'll save that recipe then," Mary nodded.

"It was wonderful," Maggie agreed.

Mary smiled and nodded, "Is there room for dessert?"

James smiled and sighed, "I'm sure I can make room."

Maggie giggled softly, before getting up. "You wait there, I'll bring it out."

James watched Maggie as she strode into the kitchen, before realising Mary was watching him. She had an odd expression on her face and he quickly looked away.

"Don't," she said softly.

"Sorry," James grimaced.

"No, I meant don't hide how you feel from me. Maggie is a beautiful woman. Besides," she smirked. "Don't you think I'd have said something when she kissed you at the front door?"

James blinked in surprise, "Ummm."

"Here we are," Maggie said, handing James a bowl of still slightly warm custard with sliced pear.

"Did you make this yourself?" James asked, scooping up some of the thick yellow liquid.

Maggie smiled, "From powder, but even that is better than the stuff in cartons."

James grinned as he made short work of his dessert, until it too was gone. This time, he waited for both ladies to finish up, before collecting their bowls. Then, without a word, he took them into the kitchen and started washing up.

"Such a gentleman," Maggie smiled, coming up behind him.

"I'm taking a shower," Mary called out, shooting them both a smile, before vanishing down the hall.

That left James with Maggie, who picked up a tea-towel and started drying the things he had washed.

"I wanted to check in," Maggie started. "I'm sure this has all been a bit of a shock and I just-"

James pulled his hands out of the water, flicked the suds away, before grabbing Maggie and kissing her firmly. She moaned in delight as James pulled away.

"I have something to tell you and Mary, about this whole thing. And I have no idea how you're going to react. So just know for now, I'm extremely happy knowing you're not mad about… About being pregnant."

"Mad?" Maggie chuckled. "James, my ex got two kids out of me, convinced me to shut up shop and then left with another woman. I don't understand how this all happened, but I feel like I've just been given part of myself back, so don't you dare think this is anything less than a miracle."

"Alright," James nodded, before going back to the dishes.

"That goes for Mary as well, so you know. She and I did a lot of talking today and she spent most of it deliriously happy. She was always a little sad when we were younger and she never seemed to settle down with anyone for long. And… Well now we know why."

"Just can't believe there are men in this world who would turn away such a beautiful woman because she couldn't have kids."

A sharp intake caught his attention and James glanced over his shoulder, to see Mary. Her hair was slicked back from the water and she was wrapped in a towel. It was the tremble in her lip that shook him. Turning, James took the tea towel offered by Maggie and dried his hands, before stepping up to Mary.

"I don't know where this is all going," James smiled, still a little unsure. "But what we have, or had. I don't want it to stop."

"Maggie," Mary smiled, "Go take a shower." Maggie smiled back a little nervously, before nodding and heading off. Mary leaned into James's shoulder and sighed softly. "She was my best friend for many, many years. Thank you for bringing her back into my life."

"Ummm," James hugged her somewhat awkwardly. "I suppose you're welcome."

She lifted her head and kissed James softly, before stepping back. "Finish up here, then come meet me in the bedroom."

James nodded as Mary smiled and turned away. James for that matter, sighed and tried to ignore his raging erection as he finished the dishes in record time. As he put the last dish in the cupboard after drying, he gave the benches a quick wipe down, and headed for the bedroom. As he passed the bathroom, the door was open and there were signs of recent use, so rather than risk embarrassing someone, he knocked on the door.

"We're decent!" Mary called.

James smiled, and opened it, stepping into the room and froze in place. Mary was beaming from ear to ear in bed. But it was Maggie's nervous grimace beside her that James wasn't expecting.

"Come on," Mary gestured. "It's late and we didn't organise a suite for Maggie."

"Oh," James nodded. "Right, I'll um… I'll refund your stay then."

"That's very kind of you," Maggie said in a quiet voice.

James nodded and stripped to his underwear, before slipping into the bed beside them. Maggie watched him approach nervously, as Mary smiled and sat herself up on an elbow. James gulped seeing Mary's breasts and his thoughts immediately turned to Maggie.

"I can't believe how nervous I am," Maggie trembled.

"You can back out," Mary said quickly. "I won't hold it against you and neither will he, I'm sure."

"No… I… I want this," Maggie nodded.

"What are you talking about?" James frowned.

But Mary leaned over and met Maggie's lips with a deep kiss. Maggie shifted in the bed and started to moan softly and James's eyes almost fell out when he spotted the shape of Mary's arm. Mary released Maggie's lips and they stared into each other's eyes for a moment.

"I've missed you," Mary said softly.

"I've missed you too," Maggie said with a tremor.

The cause of her tremor was the movement of Mary's hand as she lifted her fingers and started licking them clean. Maggie stared wide eyed and took deep breaths as Mary cleaned her fingers with her tongue.

"I've missed this taste," Mary smiled. Then she glanced at James, "She gets kinda loud sometimes, you may want to distract her."

"You're not?" Maggie squeaked as Mary slipped below the covers. "Mary! OH!"

Maggie arched her back for a moment and let out a loud squeal. She grabbed at the sheets and gripped them tightly. As Maggie ran out of breath, James heard Mary moan beneath the covers and quickly took Maggie in his arms. As he pulled her close, Maggie slammed her mouth into his. She moaned into his mouth and James held her close. Running his hands over her skin, James assaulted her senses.

Running his fingers over her skin, he felt every twitch and every shudder from the contact, even as she writhed and shuddered from what Mary did to her. Pulling away from her mouth, Maggie had a small frown on her face, like she was concentrating. But her eyes were rolled back as she gasped in pleasure.

"Is that good?" He asked, cupping one of her breasts.

"Yessss," Maggie moaned.

"How long has it been?" James asked, bending down and kissing her nipple. "How long since you've had a woman go down on you?"

Maggie trembled and bit her lip as she climbed towards her orgasm. "Years," she grunted. "College."

"Best cunt I've ever tasted," Mary chimed in, before redoubling her efforts.

"Oh fuck," Maggie trembled.

Arching her back, James collected her lips as she slammed into her orgasm like a freight train. Mary took no prisoners, continuing her torment, even as Maggie shook violently and her legs kicked in a desperate attempt to pull away from such extreme sensations.

"James!" Maggie begged, "She won't stop!"

James grinned at her conflicted expression. He knew she was still loving this. Mary seemed to know as well as she continued going down on her old friend. Sitting up, James straddled her chest, even as she pouted up at him.

"You're so mean," Maggie grumbled, even as she gripped his cock with both hands.

"Do you want to stop?"

The glare she shot him was a split second before she yanked his hips forward, so she could take him into her mouth. James smiled as she moaned around his cock. So he set the pace, slowly fucking her mouth. He didn't go very deep, not wanting to choke her. Maggie for that matter sucked and licked with each small thrust of his hips. With James's cock in her mouth, and Mary's tongue on her clit, she was reduced to small grunts of animalistic pleasure.

"You're so beautiful," James sighed.

Maggie snapped back to attention, looking up at James. The young man, who through some miracle act, had gotten her pregnant. Redoubling her efforts, James cringed as the pleasure ramped up.

"Maggie," James grunted. "I'm gonna cum."

If anything, her mouth got that much wilder, before she started to tremble and gasp. As her body shook beneath him, James realised she was cumming and swiftly joined her. Pumping his seed into her mouth, Mary sucked on the head of his cock like a straw, milking his pleasure even as Mary milked her own. When James finally finished, he slipped off her as Mary scrambled up.

One moment, Maggie was laying there, tasting James's seed, and the next, Mary's tongue was in her mouth. Maggie moaned in pleasure as they fought over his offering. Mary's squeak caught her attention. James, seeing them fight over what was in Maggie's mouth, was as hard as he was earlier. Swinging around them both, he quickly located Mary's drooling pussy and slid his cock into her from behind.

Maggie, realising what was happening, continued kissing her oldest friend as she bucked and shuddered above her. Their duel over his seed reduced to simply swapping and sharing it between one another. James, leaned on Mary's ass, forcing her crotch to crotch with Maggie. Each thrust of his hips caused them to rub the very tops of their mounds together and Maggie began to rock her hips into the stimulation.

Pulling his cock free of Mary, he angled it down and plunged straight into Maggie. Mary, feeling Maggie tense beneath her, realised immediately what had happened. So she rocked her hips, driving her crotch into Maggie's as best she could. When she felt Jame's cock slam back inside her, she almost screamed into Maggie's mouth at the sudden onslaught of pleasure. And as quickly as it arrived, he pulled free and it was Maggie's turn to squeal.

James grit his teeth as he swapped and changed between the two women. A few strokes inside Maggie and he felt her pussy begin to clench in anticipation for her next orgasm. So he yanked free and pushed himself into Mary. Thrusting into Mary, she began to tense and shudder, so he pulled free and slid back into Maggie. Maggie and Mary for that matter were equally going insane. With each swap, they climbed higher and higher to their individual climaxes.

"Fuck, you both feel so good," James grit his teeth.

Pulling his cock back out of Mary, he shifted to slide it back into Maggie, and missed. His cock, slid up from her pussy, and aided by a combination of both their juices, was steered between both their mons. The length of his cock dragged along both their clits for several moments and Mary, alongside Maggie cried out in pleasure as they came. James, recognising a good thing, thrust a few more times as their pleasure built to a crescendo, before gritting his teeth and cumming between the two of them. Even as his legs wobbled and his thrusts became erratic, Maggie and Mary humped their hips back and forth, massaging their clits and his cock until he pulled it free due to sensitivity.

Sitting back, James took several deep breaths as he watched the last of the tiny visual pulses of their pussy muscles. Pulling away, Mary grinned down at Maggie, before moving back down.

"You swallow that one, I'll get this one."

Maggie groaned as Mary began to lap at her stomach. With each lick, she got lower and lower and Maggie's moans got louder and louder until Mary's tongue started to trace around Maggie's labia. James was about to get back into the action, seeing Mary's ass wiggling in the air, but Maggie suddenly sat up, pulling Mary up as she did.

Mary suddenly looked concerned, "Hey, are you-MMMmmm."

Maggie pulled away from their kiss, before she shoved Mary down beside her. "After all those years, I didn't once return the favour," she said softly.

Mary took Maggie's hand and gave it a squeeze. "We spoke about it. I wanted to, you weren't sure. Going down on you was hot, but I never held it against you that you never returned the favour."

Maggie smiled and kissed down Mary's neck. James was frozen in place, watching the sapphic pair before him. He caught the wink Maggie shot him and gulped as his cock came back to full mast. Maggie lapped at Mary's stomach. She kissed, nibbled and made sure to visibly swallow every last drop of cum she found, before pausing right over Mary's clit.

"You don't-Fuckholyshitfuck," Mary gasped.

Maggie moaned as she gently sucked on her first clitoris and James got to his knees. Mary was gasping in pleasure as Maggie went down on her for the first time. It was as James straddled her chest, she realised their positions had swapped. Opening her mouth, she moaned as James slid half his length, comfortably into her mouth. James grinned down at the beautiful woman as she mouthed and licked his cock, while he took his pleasure with her mouth. The look in her eyes as she stared up at him, made him smile. She looked so cute and innocent as James began to spasm, filling her mouth like he had Maggie's. And as he got off, as Maggie moved up to kiss her, Mary couldn't help but shudder as her oldest friend kissed her, while her newest slid his cock back inside her.

CHAPTER FIVE

"It makes sense," Maggie said softly as she picked at her eggs.

Mary nodded slowly, "When you have eliminated all which is impossible, then whatever remains, however improbable, must be the truth."

"Arthur Conan Doyle?" Maggie asked, and Mary nodded her confirmation.

"I just can't believe that you're not questioning my sanity right now," James sighed. "I questioned it when Baal told me last night."

We were sitting in the main dining room. After waking up, none of us felt like cooking breakfast. And as the boss, James had to qualms about making sure his staff were fed. So as the kitchens opened, James, Maggie and Mary had piled in for fresh eggs, bacon and whatever else was put out today.

"James, I regrew my womb AND fell pregnant," Maggie smirked. "I honestly couldn't tell you which of those stories sounds more impossible, but I have to face reality."

"She's right," Mary smiled at him. "Her womb, my ovaries,

both of us pregnant. The only thing I'm worried about is that other thing," she sighed.

I sighed and nodded my head. The catch in all this. "I really don't know what to do about that either."

"What if…" Maggie paused, before taking Mary's hand. "What if you do it?"

James shook his head, "I couldn't do that to you. I always thought I'd meet the right woman, we'd fall in love. Bring them home to meet mum and dad, then get married and have two or three kids. Now…" James sighed. "Now I don't want any of that. I… I was serious about not knowing what was going to happen, just… I wanna be a good dad and I want both…" James trailed off, realising how crazy he was being.

"Please finish that sentence," Mary murmured softly.

"I want both of you… With me…" James sighed, slumping into his chair. He was being crazy, he knew it. Best case scenario, Mary would stick around while Maggie would visit occasionally. He'd pay whatever child support he needed and-

"I'm in," Maggie said softly.

"That's three aye's," Mary smiled.

James almost fell off his chair, he straightened so quickly. "What?"

They both giggled at him, before reaching over and taking a hand each. "You gave me a child," Mary said softly. "I'm willing to give this a try if you are. I practically live here now anyway and you don't do anything too annoying."

"If Mary can handle you, I'm sure you can't be that bad," Maggie said before frowning. "Besides, you can't be as bad as my ex."

"I did warn you," Mary gave her a nudge and Maggie nodded her head.

"I know, but I was young and stupid and he spent a lot of time making me feel things that weren't real."

"How do you know, that isn't what's going on here?" James asked.

Both the ladies looked at him and smiled. "Just asking that question makes you a better man than he was," Maggie said softly.

"So, we're in agreement," Mary smiled. "We'll give this whole thing a try. Reevaluate in a month, see how we all stand?"

"Agreed," Maggie said with a smile.

James just blinked at them both, before pinching his arm to be certain. Rubbing the sore spot, he ignored the ladies as they gave him a bemused look and nodded, "Agreed."

"Now, for my idea," Maggie smiled.

"No," James shook his head, "I'm not going to go around sleeping with random women to get them pregnant. That's not fair on you, or them."

"Sperm donation," Maggie continued, as Mary's expression shifted from concern into confusion. "How does donating sperm make everyone feel?"

"I… Don't see any harm," Mary nodded.

"That could work," James nodded.

"Unfortunately it would not," Baal said, appearing with a plate of food, despite nobody seeing him even enter the room. "May I take a seat, I may be of assistance if you are taking this seriously."

James glanced at Mary and Maggie. Mary looked suspicious, but Maggie looked thoughtful. "Sure Baal, take a seat."

"Thank you," the older man smiled.

"Why didn't you tell him beforehand?" Mary asked.

Baal's characteristic smile dropped, "That's a fair question. But, imagine if I had? Whether he believed me or not, do you think he would have slept with the two of you?"

"You manipulated me," James frowned.

Baal just nodded, "I'm sorry James. But it's a lot easier to explain a situation while you're staring at the evidence."

"Did you," Maggie suddenly looked concerned. "Did you make, this all-"

"No," Baal growled quickly. "All my power lies in fertility. I make the bits work, I don't make them WANT to work."

"I could feel them," James frowned. "All the spots on her that felt sore, that she wanted touched, or rubbed. It was almost like instinct."

"But you're responsible for doing so," Baal shrugged. "Understand ladies, James, the senior, was one of the best friends I've had since coming to earth. If I could manipulate minds, he would still be alive. Whatever you felt when he put his hands on you, was all him. I just gave him a couple extra tools to find the good spots."

"You owe me a massage," Mary grumbled.

"Oh, it was heavenly," Maggie sighed dreamily.

James grinned despite himself as Baal was back to his characteristic smile. "Right, thanks Baal."

"You're welcome James," he smiled back.

"Now," James frowned. "Where were we?"

"Sperm donation," Mary offered, giving James a small glare.

"Oh yes," Baal cut in. "The curse is a bodily one. Sperm donation won't allow for the… Magic, to work. He has to do it himself."

"That… Is still manageable," Maggie frowned.

"Maggie, he already said he doesn't want to go around impregnating random women," Mary sighed.

"So what if it's intentional?" Maggie asked. "I came in as a VIP, by sheer chance it was James that stepped through that door. What if we advertise a special VIP package? I'll put up my medical record with my details redacted. We advertise it as a homeopathic procedure to older ladies, get clients to sign a non-disclosure then give them the options."

"Options?" James asked.

"Option one, they leave," Maggie said softly. "Option two, they cough up a massive fee, then you rub them down, and make em feel good."

"That would certainly work," Baal nodded. "Not sure I like the amount of paperwork I'll be filing though."

"Are you doing the books?" Maggie asked.

"Unfortunately," the older man sighed.

"James, sell me twenty percent of the business," Maggie said immediately.

"What-"

"Twenty percent," she interrupted. "As a part owner, I'll pay to have this place refurbished. We'll upgrade your suite with a nursery and some other things, that way it's comfortable for Mary and I to stay."

"I think I'll leave you to it. Clients will be arriving soon, so I'll handle arrivals," Baal got up and returned his dirty plate to the kitchen.

"Not that I'm prying, but how can you afford all this?" James asked.

"Background in finance," Maggie shrugged. "I dealt with all sorts of things for some upscale schmuck who replaced me for a younger model."

"Is that what happened?" Mary asked.

Maggie nodded, "Yup, bastard didn't even have the balls to fire me. He just hired a new secretary and got her to hand me the transfer paperwork. So I quit and made him pay out my long service, and my other benefits. I've been living in a small apartment out of a suitcase while I figured out where I went next. And," she smiled," I suppose that's here."

"I don't know what to say," James said, looking at them both.

"Is there anything to say?" Mary asked.

Swallowing nervously, James sighed. "Alright. Twenty percent it is."

"Great," Maggie said, putting down her fork. "I'll start the refurb now, the paperwork will take a little time, but the sooner we get this place up to scratch the better."

"I've got my first client in ten," Mary said, checking the time on her phone.

"Alright, I'll head to my office then," James supplied.

"I'll be coming with you," Maggie smiled.

Mary giggled as she stood, "Don't go getting into any mischief," she leaned down and kissed Maggie, who blushed fiercely. "What's with the face?"

"I… Ummm," Maggie twitched for a moment, "We're in public and-"

"Oh," Mary frowned for a moment. "Okay, well-"

Maggie kissed her firmly. Not the small chaste peck that Mary had just given her. James could see their tongues rolling together for a few moments, before they pulled away. And now they both blushed furiously.

"I've never kissed a woman in public," Maggie said softly. "But we're partners now, so I WILL be getting used to it."

"O-okay," Mary mumbled.

"Now go kiss our man, while I take the plates."

Ten minutes later, James was checking his emails while Maggie made several calls. An hour after that, James and Maggie met with the first of the contractors. She'd found three to come out and provide quotes. The first to arrive was a young man in a suit. James and Maggie walked him through the spa. He kept up a long line of chatter, emphasising what kind of services they could accomplish within certain timeframes. By the end of their tour, James was just about ready to sign on, when Maggie sat them down in James's office.

"Alright, Mr. Tenor," Maggie smiled.

"You can call me David," the man smiled brightly, and suddenly James liked him a little less.

"Very well David," Maggie grinned. "Your suppliers, where are they located?"

David frowned for a moment, "Our suppliers are overseas. They source the finest materials and have it shipped in. So we already have everything on hand, it's just a matter of bringing it out."

"So you don't have any locally supplied wood, for example?"

"Ah, no. I'm afraid not."

Maggie frowned, "Mr Tenor, I'm sure you're aware that this spa is located within a natural reserve. Using local supplies would be the best option, at the very least for decor."

"It would be possible to stain anything we brought in," David continued. "If you're worried about the aesthetics, we can spend a bit of time testing, making sure we got the colours right."

Maggie nodded, "I will take that into consideration Mr Tenor. Thank you for your time."

"I see," Mr Tenor frowned. "In that case, I shall just bill you for my time. Should you decide to go with our company, we will comp the charge."

"Bill, Mr Tenor?" Maggie frowned. Taking out her phone, she fiddled around for a moment, before tapping the screen and placing it on the desk.

"Alright, you're booked in for an appointment at noon," Mr Tenor's voice said from the device.

"Great, now are there any additional costs, call out fees for example?" Maggie's voice asked.

"We don't charge-"

Mr Tenor leaned over and tapped the screen, closing the app. "I will be going now," he said rather stiffly.

"Have a wonderful day," Maggie called out.

The man didn't respond as he closed the door behind him. James sighed, before looking at Maggie. "Explain that to me?"

"They're the largest business in the area. If we wanted something done quickly and efficiently, they probably would have been the best. But his reluctance to specify where their materials came from, tells me it's likely the finest materials produced in some sweatshop."

"And the recording?"

Maggie shrugged, "I record any conversation over the phone. You'd be surprised how often things like this come up."

James nodded, "Alright, what's next?"

"Next," Maggie said, standing up. "We have about an hour until the next one arrives."

James nodded and then gaped as Maggie lifted her skirt over her hips. He could see the perfect shape of her bare ass and grew hard in an instant, knowing she wasn't wearing any panties. Standing, James stepped around the desk and kissed her fiercely. She moaned in appreciation and allowed James to steer her into the desk. Sliding his hands down to cup her ass, James lifted her onto the edge and pushed her legs open. With a final kiss, James got to his knees and took in the sight of Maggie's swollen pussy.

Maggie bit her lip as she watched James get on her knees. She loved how Mary went down on her, and she looked forward to getting lots of practice in herself. There was something otherworldly as James's tongue pressed between her labia. She twitched and bit her lip as the firm muscle swirled around. Looking down at him, her breathing became heavier as he pulled his tongue away and licked his lips.

Maggie bit her own lip to stop herself from crying out as James licked her from asshole to clit. She breathed heavily as she felt him open her pussy with his fingers. Then his mouth closed over her clit and Maggie jerked on the desk. The firm suction over her sensitive organ had Maggie trembling as she gripped the edges of the desk. His fingers pushed up inside her and curled towards her g-spot. She could feel the ball of heat in her core rolling around and Maggie knew what was about to happen.

"J-James!" She squeaked. "Stop!"

"Mmm?!" James mumbled around her clit, making Maggie gasp.

"Stop, or I'm going to make a mess!"

James paused. Glancing up, he could see her internal turmoil. He knew she felt good and he had a hunch of what her concern was. And that was exactly what he wanted. With an emphatic "Mm'mm." He continued.

Maggie gasped as he redoubled his efforts. His fingers rubbed up inside her, making her pussy clench over them. His mouth stayed wrapped around her clit, sucking her flesh gently. It was the introduction of his tongue, swirling over the head that finally pushed her over the edge. In a last ditch effort to spare him, Maggie tried to pull her legs closed, while pushing on his forehead. James used his spare arm to hug around her ass on the desk, and hold himself in place.

"James!" Maggie cried.

As Maggie's pussy clamped down over his fingers, James just kept the pace going. He felt the first major pulse of his pleasure roll right through her. It came with a jet of hot fluid, but James didn't care. As she sprayed down the front of his shirt, James kept up the suction on Maggie's clit. The hand on his forehead slipped around behind, holding him in place. Which was exactly what James wanted as he continued pleasuring her through her own orgasm.

As the spasms on his fingers began to dull, James released her clit with a soft pop. Maggie gasped as he stood and she leaned into him to apologise. He'd licked her after squirting that first time, but she didn't know how he felt about her squirting while he was down there. Looking up, James's mouth collected her own, as his cock slid up inside her. Her gasp was the only thing that escaped as he buried himself to the hilt in a single thrust.

"James!" Maggie whimpered.

"It's so fucking hot when you do that," James growled, biting the side of her neck.

"W-wha?"

"I've never been with a woman who squirted before," James continued, thrusting his cock inside Maggie's pregnant pussy. "Do you squirt all the time?"

"No," Maggie whimpered in confusion and pleasure as he fucked her.

"That's a shame," James grunted, speeding up. "I'm going to have to practice a lot to find out how to make you."

"G-spot," Maggie said, before gritting her teeth.

"Oh?" James paused.

Pulling his cock free, James kissed Maggie as she frowned at him. She allowed him to help her off the desk. Turning her around, James leaned her over the desk, before pulling her ass back out towards him.

"No, James!" Maggie grumbled.

This time he stopped, "Are you saying no because you don't want it? Or because you don't want me to make you squirt?"

Maggie whimpered softly and leaned on his desk. "My ex-husband hated when I squirted, I don't-"

The swat of a hand on her ass made Maggie jump. "Weren't you listening? You squirting is fucking hot! The idea of your soppy, pregnant pussy, squirting over my cock is… Is…" James couldn't quite get the words out, so he just snarled and pushed his cock into her. "Just be a good girl and squirt on my cock while I fuck you."

James used long strokes, pulling his cock all the way out, before pushing back in. With each stroke, his cock pressed into her g-spot and Maggie was left whining as he did so. She had always liked when her ex had taken charge, but this was something else. Before, it had been about being subservient to his needs. And that hit her spot on more than one occasion. But this was something else. James wasn't just fucking her for the sake of fucking her. He was fucking her in a way he knew would drive her crazy. Being pregnant with his child at the same time, just heightened everything she was feeling.

"God your pussy feels good," James grunted. "I can't wait until after the birth. I'm going to fuck you just like this, to get you pregnant a second time."

As the words sunk into her brain, Maggie hit her climax. Pressing her face into the desk, she cried out softly as her fingernails scraped on the wooden surface. James had no intention of stopping. He kept going as her legs trembled and her pussy throbbed. This time as she felt the heat inside explode, she didn't try to hide it. Beaming widely, she arched her back, letting his cock get better traction over her g-spot.

"Fuck, I love you!" Maggie squealed and gushed between her legs.

James's first reaction at the squirt was to grin. Her words hit him like a freight train. Grabbing her, he pulled her up and pinned her against his chest as he emptied himself inside her. The natural motions of their heavy breathing milked their combined orgasms, even as her pussy muscled practically milked the head of his cock.

"I love you too," James sighed. "Both of you."

"Hmmm?" Maggie frowned, turning her head.

James had felt her when she came in and as Mary's arms wrapped around them both, she smiled. "I love you too. You fuck like a machine, love me like a queen and you're breeding us like animals."

"That sounds so dirty," Maggie groaned.

"Well get our man to pull his cock out, so I can clean you up."

Maggie had finally stopped blushing every time James looked at her, as they walked around the property for the second time that day. Only this time, James was conscious of the tiny squelch from between Maggie's thighs.

The man who'd come in, an older gentleman in his sixties or early seventies, had taken a look at each of them, before shaking Maggie's hand first. "Joseph," he introduced himself. He was a local that was actually our first pick, but he had his granddaughter's recital to attend, so he'd only made it out after that. And James was pretty sure both he and Maggie didn't hold it against him.

"So, the good news," Joseph started as he ran his hands over the walls of a cabin. "Most of the wood here is still in good condition. I'd say this place was built from the trees that were here when they started."

"And the bad news?" Maggie asked.

"Gonna have to get my daughter out here to do some landscaping," he said, before gesturing to a few spots. "I'm no expert, but I'm pretty sure you'll find that when it rains, the water pools up. Then there's the trees themselves," he pointed at one beside the cabin. "They shouldn't be touching the structure or leaves marks, traps water and can cause damage over time. So that'll put my quote up to cover her expenses."

"Your daughter runs a landscaping business?"

"Mhm," he sighed. "People give her trouble for being a

woman. But she's a damn sight better than most of the others around here."

"We're looking for a landscaper," Maggie smiled. "If you could give her a call, we would love to hear from her."

Joseph shot Maggie a smile, before taking out his phone and wandering off.

"Your feelings on this one?" James asked.

"Old school, expensive, says what he means and doesn't like half-assed jobs."

"So-"

"He's hired, and if his daughter is half the woman he is, she is too."

James nodded. Maggie was far more experienced with this than he was, and he wasn't afraid to admit it. Twenty minutes later, a second vehicle pulled up and a tall, broad shouldered woman stepped out. She gave Joseph a hug and kiss on the cheek, before doing the exact same thing he had, by shaking Maggie's hand first.

"Sorry sir," the woman smiled at James. "But she's obviously the one in charge here."

Immediately James remembered the way she begged, before he allowed her to suck his dick, as Mary ate her creampie.

"Certainly in this instance she is," James smiled as Maggie blushed, knowing exactly what he meant.

An hour later, James shook Joseph and Sara's hands before they both left, contract in hand. Maggie was impressed with both of them. They seemed less concerned about timeframes and performance, and more on making sure things were done correctly. Joseph's team was going to start at the foyer, and work their way back with minor changes as to material availability. Sara on the other hand, was coming back with her survey equipment to mark out where the drainage should go. Then things got quite busy.

Mary took a few days to officially move in, while Maggie already had her suitcase in the trunk of her car. Both kept their leases going for the short term at least. But James was confident they wouldn't be renewing after the third week he woke up to them using his shoulders as pillows. Life had drifted back into the realm of normality for the most part. As the refurbishment went on, word got out into the town. Some of the workmen that Joseph hired came back on their days off for massages. Others brought their families. When James heard that a young man was getting married, he handed over a bunch of VIP packages for his fiance and her bridesmaids. After James and Mary had finished with the five ladies, they'd lorded their treatment over social media and fresh clients rang every day.

Business was booming. Money was being made. The spa was almost completed and James had already prepared gifts for Joseph and his daughter. Maggie had even started buying the surrounding land, in the hopes to keep it out of the hands of developers. They even had a kids section put in. With the cabins, there was a small market for families to come stay. Parents got their spa treatments, while the kids had access to a pool, arcade and a playground. An area had been set out in a clearing with a projector at one end, where they played movies when the evenings were good. That had led to a small delegation of locals coming up from the nearby town on a regular basis. So now the kitchens operated as a small restaurant. If you wanted a four course meal, you had to come inside. But if you wanted chips, pizza or something to snack on for the movie, a waiter could bring it outside for you to enjoy.

And with all this going on, the business was booming, reviews were coming in, money was climbing despite their fees not increasing. There was just one problem.

"You need to start taking this seriously," Baal said, sitting across from James in his office.

"We're running it as a business," James sighed. "Trying to convince women I can get them pregnant isn't easy." Baal nodded, but there was a knock on the door. "Come in!"

It opened quickly and Maggie stepped in, before spotting Baal. "Am I interrupting?"

"Not at all," Baal smiled. "I'll just be going."

James watched the older man step out of the room, before Maggie closed the door and gave him a nervous smile. "We've got one."

"Oh," James frowned. "We were actually just talking about that."

"I figured," Maggie nodded. "The client's name is Henrietta Bliss, she's forty-eight-"

I waved for Maggie to stop. "Just a name is fine. I don't need all their details. It's probably best if I view it as a transaction, rather than anything more… Intimate."

Maggie nodded, "Well she's an old friend of mine. She and her husband have been trying for years with no success."

"Married?" James asked.

Maggie nodded, "Yes, I told her a little. She and her husband discussed it. Doctors aren't sure what the problem is and they've spent a lot of money trying. So they consider this a sort of last resort."

"Right," James sighed. "When do they get here?"

"Tomorrow morning, they're staying one night." A knock on the door caught both their attention. Maggie simply turned and opened it. "Mary, what's wrong?"

Mary leaned in and pecked Maggie's lips, before turning to James. "Sara's strained something in her back."

"Is she okay?" James asked, getting to his feet.

"She's fine," Mary smiled. "Little tender in a couple places. Apparently she slipped while lifting something. I was wondering if you would mind giving her a rub down. You've got the fancy mumbo jumbo that'll say where she's sore."

"Right, where is she?"

"Same room you met Maggie, she was just getting out of the shower when I came to get you."

"Alright," James nodded. Giving each of his ladies a kiss, James headed for the room he'd never forget.

Knocking on the door, he heard a small voice call out to come in, so he pushed it open. Sara was laying face down on the bed. "How are you feeling?"

"Oh?" Sara sat up slightly, but not enough to uncover her breasts. "I thought it was going to be Mary?"

James paused, "If you like-"

"No no," she smiled and lay back down. "You're fine. I just heard your voice and was surprised. I slipped out back while carrying a bag of sand and pulled something. I've got a massage guy I usually get to, but I was already here and Mary offered."

"That's fine," James smiled. "Let me get some oil and I'll see what I can do for you. Any preference in scent?"

"Mint if you have it," Sara replied as she shifted uncomfortably.

James nodded and sure enough, there was a bottle of oil for mint. Plucking it from the warming bath, he poured some down her back, before adding more to his hands.

"I'm going to start at the top and work down, is that okay?"

"Sure."

Nodding, James got to work. Starting at her shoulders, James wondered at the thick muscles she'd built up over the years. She was still very much all woman, but James couldn't help but admire her physique as he went. Her shoulders though, were not the problem, so after giving them a quick rub to loosen them, he moved down. At her spine, he could feel far more tension. And it got worse the further down he went. Each little problem spot got a bit of attention. Muscle by muscle, he loosened each one as Sara groaned appropriately under his care. When he finally got to her ass and felt the lack of tension, James stepped back.

"Have a bit of a wriggle, tell me how you feel?"

Sitting up, Sara twisted, oblivious to James's open stare towards her bare breasts. Like the rest of her, they were tight and firm, sitting proudly on her chest with only a hint of sag.

"Holy shit," Sara grumbled.

Turning to James, he felt a hungry gaze. James didn't have time to move as she stood, showing him her nakedness. A moment later, he was stunned as she yanked his pants down and took him in her mouth.

"Sara!" James grunted as his cock hardened and poked into the back of her throat. "What are you doing?"

Pulling off his cock with a pop, she smiled and stroked him. "Fair is fair. You made me feel good, I'm just returning the favour."

"Wait," James grunted as she took him deep in her mouth again. "Fuck, I already have someone."

Pulling away, Sara shrugged and turned James around. Pushing him backward, he bumped into the table and Sara simply pushed him up onto it. "Look, if you really want me to stop, I'll stop. But it's been a long time since a man put his hands on me."

"I could get you pregnant!" James hissed.

Sara sighed, "No, you can't."

"No, you don't understand," James grunted, as she lifted herself and rubbed her clit on his cock. "I can, I really can. There's shit going on you don't know about."

"Are you trying to tell me you have a magic penis?" Sara slowed.

"YES!" James grunted as her fingers gently stroked the underside of his cock.

Sara stopped and looked down at him for a moment. "You really think you can get me pregnant? Hell, the reason I'm single is because two husbands couldn't, what makes you special?"

"Maggie and Mary," James grunted as he felt the wetness of Sara's pussy leaking over his cock. "It'll sound crazy if I tell you, but they have proof."

Sara frowned for a moment, before patting his cock against her clit. "If... And I mean if you can get me pregnant, would you?"

"Talk to Maggie and Mary," James repeated. "Maggie's the one in charge of that side of the business, but I love them both."

In an instant, Sara looked remorseful and slipped off. "Oh shit... I'm sorry, I didn't realise."

James sighed and tried tucking away his still hard cock, "It's literally not the first time."

"Really?"

"Yeah," James growled at his disobedient erection. "That's how I have them both."

Sara nodded, "Alright... Well... For what it's worth, I'm sorry. It's... It's been a while."

James looked up at her. Despite the fact she could probably bench press him, she looked quite fragile at that moment. Stepping up, he gave her a quick hug. "I'll let them know you're coming for a chat." Pulling away, James strode over to the door and paused with his hand on the knob. "Sara?"

"Yeah?"

"You're a beautiful woman."

Stepping out of the room, he didn't see the small tear that rolled down her cheek, nor did he see her beaming smile.

CHAPTER SIX

James put down his fork and sighed. Mary gently patted his hand, while Maggie began to stack their dishes. Taking the older woman's digits James squeezed softly.

"Are you really okay with this?"

Mary smiled thinly and nodded, "I think so."

"Think?" James asked softly.

Mary stared at him for a few moments, before Maggie joined them, taking James's other hand. "What are the options?"

"You do this, or you die young," Mary muttered.

James just shook his head, "I just don't want to hurt you. Things got really intense with Sara yesterday and…"

"We'll have to speak with her about that," Maggie nodded. "But as for hurting us, James. We're not jealous teenagers. You're going to come home every night to US, kiss US, probably fuck us silly and fall asleep with US. And after we give birth, you're probably going to do it again."

"She's right," Mary smirked. "I know I got a bit jealous earlier when I found out about Maggie, but it was more about the feeling of betrayal, rather than a desire to keep you to myself."

James just looked at them both and nodded, "So for the last time, you're okay with this?"

They both leaned in as one and gave him a three-way kiss. As they pulled away, Maggie smiled. "Go have sex with my friend, make her squirm, get her pregnant, then you can tell us all about it tonight, while we take turns sliding our wet, pregnant little pussies over your fat cock."

James blinked at her for a moment, before he realised Mary was staring at her as well.

"Who taught you to dirty talk?" She asked.

Maggie shrugged, "Did it work?"

"Yup," James grimaced, thinking about the uncomfortable tight feeling in his pants.

"Good," Maggie grinned.

Pressing her lips into James's, she collected a kiss, before doing the same to Mary. With a wiggle of her fingers she stalked out of the room, giving her hips a little wiggle as she went. Mary sighed, before leaning over and collecting a kiss from James as well.

"While you're with Henrietta, I believe I'm giving her husband a massage," She smiled.

"Are you really okay with this?" James asked one final time.

Mary sighed and nodded, "Yeah, just… Please come back to us."

James frowned, before leaning in and kissing her deeply. When he pulled away, she smiled awkwardly and looked away. James cupped her cheek and gently pulled her around to face him. "I love you," he said softly. "And I'm going to breed you until you beg me to stop."

Mary snorted and giggled, "Stop it you tease."

James kissed her on the nose and stood, "Who says I'm teasing?"

With a wink, he turned on the spot and headed for the VIP rooms. It had been decided, the room where he had met Maggie that first day, was the best place for it. Kept all in one place. It meant that no matter what, there was only one place to clean. He headed straight there and pushed into the room to give it a final check over. Wiping down the massage table, despite knowing it was already clean, James busied himself dusting and wiping for the few minutes it took before he heard a knock on the door. Tossing the rag in a wash basket disguised as a bin, James pulled the door open to a smiling Maggie.

"Ah, and here's James, if you'd like to go in?"

"You go, I'll be next door," a bored voice said.

James caught a glimpse of what must have been Henrietta's husband as he walked off and left his wife with Maggie. The woman, James was surprised to see, was small, mousy haired with thick coke bottle glasses. Her wispy, long hair had streaks of silver. She wore a plain apron-style dress with flats and James knew immediately she was extremely nervous.

"Now, she's given me a copy of her doctor's certificate. She's been briefed," Maggie said softly. "And Henny, please relax. James is a wonderful lover."

"Okay," Henny squeaked softly.

"Why don't you come in?" James offered.

Standing aside, Henny smiled nervously at Maggie and stepped into the room. James smiled at Maggie's quick thumbs up, before closing the door. Turning back to Henny, he paused as she folded the dress over her arm, wearing nothing but a pair of panties and her shoes.

"Oh," James gaped, trying not to let his eyes wander over her curves. She was a petite thing, but she was definitely all woman. "I was going to offer to leave while you got comfortable."

"Why?" She frowned nervously. "You're just going to fuck me aren't you?"

"Ummm," James paused. "I could, if that's what you want?"

She nodded and moved over to the massage table. Without a second thought, she dropped onto her elbows and stood with her legs slightly apart. James frowned for a moment, before stepping up behind her.

"Just push them down when you're ready," she said in a tone that told James, she really wasn't into this.

"Look, Henny," James frowned. "Do you want this?"

"I…" She sighed. "Yes, I want this. I promised my husband a family and everything we've tried has failed. If… If this works, it'll be everything."

Nodding James stepped up as he unzipped his fly. Fishing his cock out of his pants, he frowned at the petite woman bent over before him. Reaching up, he took the sides of her panties and pulled them down so they draped around her ankles. From here, he could see the pout of her pussy between her legs and felt himself firming. There was just one issue.

"Do you… Want some foreplay maybe?"

"Oh," Henny sighed. "Yes, my husband has this issue sometimes." Turning around, she looked down at James's erection and stopped. "Is this a joke?"

"N-no," James murmured. He was feeling rather conflicted about the whole thing. She was nervous, but abrasive in how she acted. James just couldn't get a read on her, but she clearly didn't want him touching her any more than necessary. "Lubrication, we need some lubrication."

"Don't you have some massage oils or something?"

James nodded as Henny turned back to the table and got

back in position. James went over to the warming bath and plucked out the unscented. It was the safest bet if she had allergies, but the oil itself was harmless. Pouring a little on his hands, James placed the bottle on the massage table. Rubbing his cock, he gave it a few strokes, before pressing his fingers between Henny's legs. She squirmed slightly and made an annoyed sigh, but allowed the action. James just kept quiet and hoped this could be over quicker than he was expecting it to be. Taking his cock, he steered it between her legs.

"Ready?" She asked in a flat tone.

"Yep," James replied, equally flat.

Rubbing his cock through her labia experimentally, Henny made a noise and bent over a little further. Not that it was entirely needed, but he did appreciate the help. Pressing his cock to her entrance, James pressed part way in. Removing his hand, James took Henny by the hips and slowly pushed half his length inside her. When he got to the halfway point, James reversed and pulled back out, before sliding back in. He kept the strokes slow and shallow, aiming to make it as pleasurable for her as he could. Henny on the other hand, remained silent and still as she allowed him to touch her.

After his dozenth stroke, James could feel the lubrication between them and he deepened his strokes. Now he fucked her with most of his length. It wasn't a hard fuck, but just enough that his crotch gently brushed her ass, before he retreated. Her pussy was wet and gripped him eagerly, despite her lack of any reaction.

Henny on the other hand, was going out of her mind. She thought he was using his thumb for a moment. But when his hands touched her hips, she realised the impossibly large thing pushing into her was in fact his penis. She stood in shock, as the largest thing she'd ever felt pushed up inside her. It almost hurt, it was so large and the only reason she didn't cry out was the vague semblance of the occasional time she'd slipped a finger into herself. That wasn't often though. She'd shown her husband years ago, and he'd called her a whore. Since then, she'd remained chaste except for the few times a month he wanted her. She'd gotten used to it. Standing there waiting as he masturbated, before quickly forcing himself inside her to finish. It was uncomfortable, but he didn't cause any real pain. Not like this monster inside her could have, if he hadn't thought to lubricate.

"Are you okay?" James asked after a few minutes.

"Yes," she replied, trying desperately not to moan like a whore and soil her image.

The feeling of his hips slapping into her ass made her gasp softly. This was unknown territory for her. Nothing had been this deep inside her before. And before she could process what she was feeling, he pulled free and slammed his cock back inside her again. Every time his cock slammed into her, she felt something inside build. It started as a little ball of warmth. With each smack of his balls on her clit, it grew. As his hands tightened on her hips, she wondered if he was finally going to cum. She blinked, it wouldn't just run out of her, he was so far up inside her, she'd... She'd be a receptacle for him as he filled her. Trembling, that ball of warmth in her core pulsed.

James just wanted it over with. She felt good, but she just stood there, no sound, no movement. So the sudden vice-like clamp over his cock caught him by surprise. Her high pitched whimper, followed by full body spasms, slammed James into the orgasm he was pushing for. Gripping her tightly, he thrust up into her one final time, and started firing ropes of cum deep inside her. Henny rocked her hips as he body spasmed and came around him. She continued to whimper and shake even as the final spurt of his cum fired off inside her. James held her steady until she was able to stand, before slowly pulling himself free. Henny trembled and let out a small gasp as his still firm cock finally slipped out of her. Slapping a hand to her crotch, she turned around and stared at the cock jutting out in front of him.

"That was inside me?" She asked.

"Ummm," James mumbled. "Yes."

"But… It's so big?"

James blinked down at himself. "Not really, maybe a little over average, but I'm not huge." Henny just stared for a moment, until James got uncomfortable and started tucking himself away. "Look ah… There's a shower back there. Feel free to clean yourself up. Your meals here are covered by your fees. Please enjoy your stay."

With a polite smile, James turned and quickly left the room, ignorant of the confused, yet hungry glare that followed his retreat. James sighed and made his way back to his suite. Inside, he headed straight for the shower, stripping off and climbing in before the water warmed up. He stood there in the water column, shaking his head. It wasn't that he felt cheap or used, it was just that he'd never felt so… Detached before.

Meanwhile, Henny stepped out of the shower. Wrapped in a towel, she quickly redressed in the clothes she'd worn in, before taking out her phone. Opening her browser, she typed in a few words and frowned at the results. Changing a few, she got something a little closer to what she was searching for. With a disgruntled snarl, she tapped a few random links and blinked at what came up. Tapping the first video, she blinked at what came up on the screen. The sight and sounds coming from the device had her blushing and fumbling to lower the volume. Now at least she knew that the young man wasn't the odd one here. She and her husband were.

"James?" Maggie called, stepping into the suite.

He sighed while sitting on the couch. "Here love."

"You ready?"

"Ready?"

"Yeah…" she frowned. "You have three sessions, and you're coming up for the noon one."

James sighed, before nodding his head. "Right, they're… They're not all going to be like this, right?"

Maggie frowned and shook her head. "No, I figured once things started rolling, we'd stick to single sessions. Only a handful of clients a week at most, that way you can still spend time with us."

"Good," James sighed.

"Is it really that bad?"

He shook his head, "It's… It's not that it's bad. She just… Stood there, like I was checking her back for spots or something."

"Oh," Maggie frowned, thinking of the vibrant, excitable woman she knew in her younger days. Then she thought about the dismissive manner of her husband when he just walked off without a care for Mary to tend to. "Do… You want me to talk to her?"

Standing, James came over and pulled Maggie into his arms. He held her for a moment, before pulling back and pecking her lips. "No, it's not my place to give relationship advice or coach people on sex. I'm just here to provide a pregnancy. I should get used to it. Probably better this way."

Maggie smiled thinly and nodded, "Alright. I just don't want you doing anything you're not fully comfortable doing."

"You and Mary really are the best thing that ever happened to me," James smiled and kissed her again. "It'll be fine. Get this over and done with, then I get to spend time with the two yummiest mummies in my life."

Maggie grinned and nodded. "Is that a thing for you? Are you gonna get more turned on as we swell up? Our pregnant little pussies dripping and begging for your attention?"

James just blinked, before softly pulling her close. Lifting his lips to her ear he said in a soft voice, "Just because I love you, doesn't mean I'm not above spanking that pregnant ass of yours."

Slipping down, he pressed several kisses to the side of her neck, making Maggie tremble, before pulling away with a grin. Pecking her lips as she drooled a little, James turned and headed for the door.

"Promises, promises," she bit her lip.

James paused as he closed the door behind him. He wondered if he had heard what he thought he had heard. Shaking his head, he decided it needed a further conversation. But that would be later. For now, he had an obligation. Henny was waiting for him in reception, idly chatting with Baal, who looked pleased with the situation. Which also meant that she was probably already pregnant. Would be nice to know it really only took one time.

"And here's James. I'll leave you to it," Baal smiled.

"It was wonderful chatting with you," Henny smiled, before turning to James with an awkward blush. "Shall we?"

James smiled professionally, "Yes, if you'd like to follow me?"

He caught the subtle nod from Baal that confirmed his belief, before leading Henny back to the room they had started. As expected, it had been tidied by the cleaning crew. He wasn't sure who it was, it may have even been Maggie for all he knew. He just hoped they were discreet. After closing the door, he sighed, thinking about the state of the massage table.

"Should talk to Maggie about that," he mumbled.

"Sorry, what was that?" Henny asked.

"Oh nothing, just thinking we needed to update the… furniture," He stared at the blushing woman, who blushed fiercely as she stood naked before him. "Ummm… Are you ready?"

She nodded, "How… Ummm… How do you want me?"

James thought for a moment and all that came out was, "How you were before was fine."

"Oh," she said, sounding a little disappointed. "Okay."

Turning she leaned back over the massage table. From here, James could see she was at least a little aroused, going by the glistening dew on her labia. He wasn't taking any chances though. Heading for the oils, he grabbed the one from earlier, before untucking his cock. Pouring a little oil onto his hands, he massaged his length and turned back to Henny. She had shifted, leaning further onto the bed, but had raised one leg, so her knee was on the massage table, giving him a perfect view of her labia, puffy and open with arousal.

"Ummm," she mumbled. "I thought, this might be easier."

"Sure," James said a little quickly, before stepping up. "Do you mind if-"

"You can touch me," she said, cutting him off.

James nodded, before realising she couldn't see him. "Right, okay, thank you."

Reaching down, he wiped the oil between her legs, and immediately realised how useless the gesture was. She wasn't just a little damp, she was almost drooling. The heat she produced left nothing to question, and James wondered at the change in circumstances. Maybe she had really enjoyed herself after all? Perhaps she was just really nervous.

Taking his cock, he lifted it to her pussy. Pressing it to her opening, he gave a small push, only for Henny to twitch and his cock slipped out, rubbing between her labia and over her clit. Henny let out a small squeak of surprise, but James froze as he felt her hand take his cock as she repositioned him, herself.

"Ready?" James croaked.

"Yes," she replied in a small voice.

Rocking his hips, James felt the head of his cock slip into her. Her pussy opened to him like a silken glove. He felt her twitch as his cock slid inside and James gently took her hips. As he did so, she seemed to rock her hips, using the leverage of the bed and angle her ass upwards, so he could get a deeper stroke.

"So good," she mumbled in a voice too quiet for James to understand.

But he got the idea and pulled his cock almost free, before sliding it home again. This time, she let out a soft gasp. James wondered what had happened. She barely made any sign the whole time they fucked earlier, that she enjoyed anything until the orgasm at the end. Now though, she seems to be right into it from before he even had his cock inside her.

"What, ah…" James paused. "What do you like? How can I make you feel good?"

Henny gasped again as his cock pushed back up inside her. It took her a few moments to process his words as he slowly fucked her. She'd never felt like this before. She had no idea how good sex could feel. And that was the problem, "I don't know."

James slowed to a stop. "You don't know what?"

"I… I don't know any of this, it's all new."

"You've never had sex?" James asked, a little confused.

"N-no…" Henny bit her lip, wishing he'd keep fucking her. "Not like this anyway."

James frowned, then sighed… Then nodded. "Right, just… Tell me if I do something you don't like, and I'll stop straight away."

"O-okay," Henny said softly.

James sighed, wondering what it is she'd like. Running his hands up her sides, all he could feel was how tense she was. He could tell she enjoyed his touch, but she wasn't comfortable with it. So he settled for one hand on her shoulder, with the other holding her raised thigh. Rocking her gently backward, James met her reversing ass, with a thrust of his hips. Henny trembled and gasped as he started fucking her again. The hand on her shoulder made her feel like he was the one in control, but it wasn't demanding. More like, he was gently steering her towards a mutual goal. As his cock speared into her, Henny gasped and sighed, before a low moan escaped her lips. Immediately she covered her mouth in embarrassment as she waited to be called a whore.

"No," James sighed, reaching up to take her hand away from her face. "How am I supposed to know I'm doing a good job, if you're so quiet?"

Henny gasped as he started thrusting again. Each slap of his hips on her ass made her smile wider. Each thump of his balls on her clit made that ball of warmth inside grow closer.

"I don't want to sound like a whore," she mumbled.

"Whore?" James thrust deeply inside her and held her there. "Henny, I'm having sex with you for money, technically I'm the whore. But that's beside the point. A few noises of pleasure is great for my ego. It lets your partner know they're doing a good job and keeps them eager to please you. Now, moaning for the sake of moaning gets old quickly, but don't hide how you feel because you're worried. You'll feel so much better if you let yourself go and just enjoy yourself. I'm not going to judge you."

"I…" Henny frowned in confusion. "I like how your penis, feels inside me."

James blushed for a moment and smiled. "Good-"

"I want you to thrust harder," she continued.

James grinned, and tightened his grip on her shoulder and leg. Then he got to work. Pulling his cock free, he slammed it back inside her. Henny trembled and arched her back, letting out a small squeal.

"Shit," James stopped. "You okay?"

"Yes!" Henny trembled, before realising she could move and pleasure herself at the same time. "More, please more!"

James grinned, realising these sessions weren't going to be as bad as he thought they were. Gripping her tightly, James got to work. Slamming his cock into her, Henny closed her eyes and concentrated on the feeling of the cock slamming into her. Each thrust of that beautiful tool came with a small pull on her body that made her feel like she was part of the experience. For the first time, she had a man inside her, that didn't feel like it was simply an obligation.

"I," Henny grit her teeth as the heat inside her built. "I think, I… I!"

"Cum for me," James grunted, feeling his own end rushing closer. Releasing her shoulder, James leaned closer and slipped his hand between her legs. Henny froze, at the touch of his fingers on her clit. That sensitive little nub she'd ignored for years. As his hands rolled over her flesh, she opened her mouth to scream. And, despite trying to bring down the walls, no sound came out as her fingernails dug grooves in the faux leather of the massage table.

"That's it, cum for me," James crooned, feeling her clamp over his cock. "Let it all out."

Rolling her clit with his fingers, James started to pump up inside her. He thrust a few more times, trying to milk her pleasure, but settled for rubbing her clit, with himself buried deep inside. Henny on the other hand, twitched and spasmed uncontrollably. Each rotation of his wrist made her body spasm. Each spasm caused her to rock her hips as her core muscles activated. Each time she rocked her hips, that glorious cock inside her shifted, even as it pumped her full of sperm for the second time. After what felt like hours though, his hands stopped and James pulled out. Henny collapsed on the massage table, before her limp legs made her slump to the floor.

"Oh shit," James gripped the massage table to hold himself steady. "You okay?"

Henny turned on the spot and smiled up at him. Before she could speak, she realised she was a bare inch from the tip of his cock. Without thinking, she opened her mouth and sucked the head into her mouth. She'd seen it on the video, and it made her so hot to watch. And never in a million years did she think she'd ever try it.

"Shit," James grunted as she mouthed him. She was clearly inexperienced, but she made up for it with eagerness.

Henny experimented with increasing the suction. She learned quickly to keep her teeth away. But it was when she brought her tongue into things, that she heard his gasp. The combined flavours of their passion made her feel so dirty. Not only was she tasting him, but she could taste herself and the thought of pleasuring the tool that pleased her, made her ignore that baser instinct that what she was doing was wrong.

"Henny, shit," James grunted. "You're going to make me cum."

With a final suck, Henny pulled away, much to James's disappointment. But it didn't last long. This refined, older lady, on her knees, drooling between her legs onto the carpet. She opened her mouth, like she'd seen in the video and stroked his cock, keeping it aimed at her face. James shuddered and gripped the table as the first rope of his cum sprayed directly into her mouth. The taste of him must have shocked her, as she jerked her head and closed her mouth. The second shot of his cum left a line from her cheek, up over the side of her face. The third was across her forehead and over her glasses. And, she had his taste now. Opening her mouth, she dived on it, taking the final few spurts directly into her mouth as she licked and sucked the tip like a lollipop.

With a moan, James finally stopped cumming, and Henny released his cock, with a smile. He looked down at her, as she used her fingers to wipe away his sperm. Each swipe of her fingers was transferred to her mouth and James just watched in arousal as she moaned with every mouthful.

"Holy shit," James sighed.

Henny paused, before an unsure look came over her, "I'm sorry, was-"

"What on earth are you apologising for?" James snapped, before reining in his retort as Henny looked suddenly very unsure. Dropping to his knees, he took her hands and shot her a smile. "Thank you, that was wonderful."

"It… It wasn't too much?"

James grinned, "That's the first facial I've given someone, but no. It was wonderful, I just… I'm glad you're enjoying yourself. I know I'm just trying to get you pregnant, so I should try and be more professional about this. But your husband is a lucky man if you suck him half as good as you just did me."

Before Henny could respond that her husband refused to even humour the idea, she froze as James leaned in and kissed her. It was soft, chaste, more of a 'thank you' than anything filled with passion. As he pulled away and shot her a smile, Henny stared right back.

"Ummm…" She tried desperately to think of a way to ask him to kiss her again. "H-how many times do we need to do this?"

James frowned, "Technically, only once. You should be pregnant already. You're our first official client, so we planned on just being thorough and changing how we did things later."

Henny frowned and James suddenly felt like a piece of shit. "So, we don't need the three sessions then?"

"N-no," James sighed. "I'm sorry."

"James," Henny twisted her fingers together nervously. "I… I know you're with Maggie and Mary… But… Would they mind?"

James frowned, trying to work out what she was asking for. "Mind what?"

"Well, if you're right, I'm already pregnant. And now I know, the third session isn't necessary, but… Do you think we could anyway?"

James looked at the hopeful twinkle in her eye and sighed, "Go take a shower. I'll go speak to them and make sure."

"James?" Henny asked, as he went to move. Turning his attention back to her, Henny darted in and kissed him lightly. "Thank you."

"Sure," he mumbled, standing up. Tucking himself back away, he helped Henny stand, before she waddled off to the shower. James sighed, and slipped quietly from the room. And ran straight into Mary.

"Hey!" He smiled and collected a kiss.

"How was it?" Mary asked. "Maggie was saying…"

"Yeah," James nodded, "About that. We need to have a little talk."

"Me?"

"All of us," James corrected, taking her hand.

Leading her to his office, sure enough Maggie was inside. She was talking to someone on the phone. She smiled and said a few words, before putting it down.

"Hello my loves," she smiled at the pair of them. "That was

the decorator. We're having a lot of the older furniture replaced."

"Oh," James grinned. "I was going to ask about the massage tables."

"Already on it," Maggie beamed. "Now, what's up?"

"Henny," James said softly.

"Is it really that bad?" Maggie frowned.

James sighed and gave Mary's hand a squeeze. "Now it's the opposite. She got really into it, really quickly. We had a little talk at the end there and she knows she's already pregnant. But…"

"She still wants the third session," Maggie nodded.

"What do you think?" Mary asked James.

James lowered his head and sighed. "I think her husband is a bit of a wet fish. I don't think she's ever had proper sex. She got really animated this time, gave me oral and ended it with a facial."

"Wow," Maggie giggled. "This morning you were so glum about it."

"Yeah, Maggie told me," Mary offered. "That's why I was waiting outside, to make sure you were okay."

"I love you both, so very much. You know that right?" James smiled at both women, while they beamed back.

"Alright, business. How do we handle this?" Maggie asked.

"For starters, only one session from now on, per client," Mary said firmly.

"Agreed," James nodded. "From Baal's attitude, it really only takes one time. So no matter how things go, they fall pregnant and go about their lives."

"So what we need to decide is, do you sleep with Henny a third time?" Mary asked.

They sat quietly together for a few minutes and thought things over. It was Maggie who spoke up first.

"If we cancel, business would demand we offer a refund," she said slowly. "If we refund, we may have to explain to her husband why."

"Oh," Mary frowned. "Yeah, he's a bit of a sleazebag."

"What happened?" James asked carefully.

"Nothing much," Mary frowned. "He said he was just stretching, but he did touch my ass twice."

James frowned and went to get up, but Mary took his hand, and pulled him back into the chair.

"After today, he's banned from making another booking," Maggie said firmly. "Henny will be welcome, but not for the VIP service with James, unless we're all in agreement. Nobody gets a second booking unless we're ALL in agreement, no matter how much they're willing to spend."

"Agreed," James and Mary said in unison.

"But I think you should cuck him one last time. Clearly he hasn't been screwing his wife properly, so you should get into her pants one last time and make it special for her."

James just blinked at Maggie's mischievous smile and nodded, "Mary, anything you wanna add?"

"No, we're booking in for a hot stone massage later. Those rooms are pretty sound proof, but if you could try to get her nice and loud, I'll be happy with that."

"So it's agreed then," James nodded. "I'll fuck her one last time."

CHAPTER SEVEN

James sighed, thinking about what was about to happen. He had literally spoken earlier about NOT doing this very thing. Staring at the small dining table with the covered trays, he shook his head. Mary and Maggie had both agreed, so they had adjusted the last appointment to interrupt Henny's dinner with her husband. And as the knock came from the door, it was right on cue. James strode up and opened the door. Henny looked a little upset, but smiled when she saw James's suit.

"What's..." She trailed off, seeing the table set up.

"I'm sorry," James smiled. "I thought our last session together might be a little easier this way, if I interrupted anything with your husband, you can come back."

Henny froze for a moment, before smiling and stepping into the room. "I know what you're doing young man."

"Oh?" James frowned politely as he closed the door.

"I won't be one of your girls," she declared. "I'm a married woman and I will remain as such. I've been a good and faithful wife. I wouldn't be here at all except it was his wish."

"Fair enough," James smiled and led her to the table. "Then I suppose we'll just see how it all goes then, shall we?"

Pulling her chair out, Henny shot James a smile and sat. Ever the gentleman, first he pushed her seat back in, before uncovering the dish she had ordered from the restaurant. A pesto based pasta dish. She smiled as James offered her a glass of white wine to go with it, which she accepted with a smile.

"Thank you dear," she smiled.

James took his seat and uncovered his customary steak and veg. It was simple, yet delicious and exactly what he wanted. "So, what do you think of the facilities so far?"

Henny swallowed her mouthful as she thought, before smiling. "Well this room has a few fond memories. Though the massage table is a tad lumpy."

James nodded, "Maggie was on the phone to someone today, we're getting all new furniture installed."

She smiled and nodded, "Perhaps I should make another appointment when it's finished then."

James sighed, "Perhaps. But you better run it by Maggie and Mary first."

Henny paused, before taking a sip of her wine. "So it's true, you're with both of them and… They're both…"

James nodded, "Yep. Two wonderful ladies I love with all my heart. And they're both giving me children."

"I still don't quite believe it," Henny sighed. "I've tried with my husband for years, everything from traditional sperm donors to IVF. Cost us a fortune and none of it worked. Then I get a call from my old friend Maggie, who I haven't seen in a few years. I thought she was selling me snake oil at first, but then she sent me her medical records."

James paused, mid mouthful. "Yeah, I couldn't believe it either. Things in my life are very different."

"So they are," Henny smiled. "So why are you doing it?"

"Doing what?"

"Impregnating random women, is it a kink?"

I thought about it for a moment and smirked. "Don't get me wrong, nothing is more distinctly feminine than a pregnant woman. That is definitely something I'm looking forward to. But... Whether you believe me or not, I don't have much of a choice."

"What, is it like a curse or something?" She smirked.

James sighed, "Actually, yeah."

Henny frowned, "It's not going to affect the baby or-"

"No," James shook his head quickly. "No, nothing of the sort. Full disclosure. Believe me or not, I have a family curse. I will impregnate any woman I sleep with. Apparently the pregnancy released some kind of residual energy which feeds the curse. Without the pregnancy, the curse feeds on me directly. My uncle refused and that's why he died so young, leaving me as the owner of this place and the curse."

Henny blinked and looked uncomfortable for a few moments, "And, how does this curse pass on?"

"I name an heir," James sighed. "It only affects men, so if I only have daughters it dies with me and there's no more. But if I have sons, then I will have to name one."

"You won't... Name mine..."

"If it ever came to that, it would be with plenty of warning. And honestly, there's perks," James smiled. "To take full advantage of the curse, I'm going to be mostly fit and healthy my entire life and live to a ripe old age. So I'm going to be around for a long time, to have MANY children."

Henny regarded him for several moments, before turning back to her food. They ate in relative silence for the rest of the meal. James was apprehensive about what was to come, while Henny processed everything he had said. When she finally put down her fork, James smiled.

"Would you care for dessert?"

Henny giggled softly and shook her head, "No, I don't think that's necessary."

"Right," James smiled. "In that case, would you like a massage?"

She eyed him for a moment, before standing. She wore a simple dress that hung down to her ankles and in a single movement, she dropped it to the floor. She stood before him in nothing but a pair of lace underwear and she smiled at the expression on his face.

"Be honest with me for a moment."

"Sure," James nodded.

"I'm already pregnant, aren't I?"

"I believe you were pregnant after the first session. I was informed that it had been successful right before our second session."

"I'm a married woman," Henny frowned, taking her underwear in her hands. She wiggled her hips as she shifted the fabric down her thighs until they dropped to the floor where she could kick them aside. "You should be ashamed of yourself, taking advantage of an old woman's ignorance."

"I'm sorry," James frowned, slightly confused as she got onto the table completely naked. "We had no way to know it would only take the first time, and you're our first official client. We were trying to be thorough."

"Well, you better go find something floral to pour on me then," Henny said stiffly.

James nodded, and quickly got up to wash his hands. Drying them on a cloth, he found the oil he needed and got straight to work. Pouring the oil over Henny's skin, he added some more to his hands. After putting the bottle aside, he got to work. The moment he touched her, he could sense how she wanted to be touched. Despite her frigid demeanor, she was very much enjoying his attention.

Running his hands over her skin, James took his time. If

this was the last he was going to touch her, he wanted to make it memorable. He smoothed every ache, rubbed every muscle and pressed every trigger until she lay limply on the table.

"I need you to turn over, so I can do your front," James said softly.

Henny let out a soft sigh, before sitting up. Rolling into a seated position, she gestured for James to come closer, before taking his hand.

"I'm a married woman," she said softly.

"I know," James replied.

She smiled and leaned in for a kiss. James replied immediately, kissing her softly. He felt her hands move down the front of him, before she fumbled at his belt. James grabbed her shoulders and pushed her back, only to see her confused and hurt expression.

"Is this what you want?" He asked in a serious tone.

Henny looked like she was about to cry as she nodded her head, "Just once more. Please?"

Stepping back, James pulled his shirt over his head, before undoing the rest of his pants. He kicked off his shoes, and shoved the rest of his clothing off in one go, before stepping into Henny's embrace. He met her hungry kiss with one of his own. Her hands roamed over his back as he ran his hands up her sides.

"H-how do-"

"Just lay back," James said, kissing her lightly.

Henny blushed, but shifted around to lay on the massage table. James climbed on after and looked down at her drooling pussy. She blushed and went to close her legs, but James quickly moved up and laid his body over hers. Instead she was left moaning softly as James kissed up the side of her neck. He supported his weight on his elbows, pushing his arms under her back and neck, so he could cradle her against him.

"What are you doing?" She asked as she panted with need.

James just smiled and pecked her lips. "I'm giving you something to remember me by."

Slipping one arm out from under her, James made sure to cradle Henny's head as he reached down between them. His fingers lightly brushed her sensitive clit making her squirm slightly as he stared into her eyes. She clearly didn't need any additional foreplay and James suddenly had a strong urge to have her. Taking his cock in hand, James steered himself until he felt her wet labia part over the head of his cock.

"I've never," she whimpered.

"Never what?"

"Always... Always from behind, I-"

"James kissed her. He kissed her deeply, but softly. Allowing her to control the pace of things. Holding her in place, James pulled his arm out from between them and wrapped her up as he had before. Then after shuffling his knees up slightly, James pulled away from the kiss as Henny stared up at him.

As he stared into her eyes, she smiled softly, before gasping loudly as he pushed inside her. Henny trembled and her legs opened, welcoming the intrusion into her.

"Oh god!" She gasped.

James smiled and kissed her until she fell silent. Her arms still clung to him like a dying woman. So James pushed the remainder of his cock inside with a single thrust. Her gasp was muffled by their kiss and her legs snapped shut over his hips, so James knew she had enjoyed that. So he made this session soft. Gently rocking his body against her, Henny whimpered and moaned into his mouth. James just kissed her, enjoying the sensation as her pussy pulsed around him, already aching for its first release.

"Cum for me," James whispered as their lips parted. "Cum for me, then keep cumming. This is all for you."

"Oh," Henny whimpered. "Oh, please, harder?"

"No my dear," James smiled and kissed down the side of her neck. "I'm not going to change a thing," he said, gently rocking his cock into her willing pussy. "You're just going to have to learn to cum around me."

"O-oooh," Henny panted.

James smiled, and gently bit the side of her neck. Not hard enough to leave a mark, but enough that her entire body tensed for a moment as she gasped and began to tremble.

"Oh, please?" She begged as he released his jaw.

"No," James smiled, kissing her again. "This is no sprint, it's a marathon. One I am hoping to savour for a while yet."

"You're a bad man," Henny groaned as she slumped back and rocked her hips up against him.

James kept up the slow deliberate pace. The only change he made was to ensure he ground his pubic bone into Henny's mons with each thrust. The firm pressure on her clit must have been enough as she suddenly gripped him tightly.

"That's it," James crooned into her ear. "You just cum, while I keep fucking you."

Meanwhile next door, Mary was frowning at the man on the table. Mr Bliss as he liked to be called was completely nude. Not that being nude on a massage table was completely unheard of. He'd attempted to pout cutely when she'd covered his lower half with a towel when he rolled over.

"That's so good," he murmured as Mary rubbed his shoulders. "You'd make a man very happy one day."

Mary froze at his words and frowned. Right as a soft "OHMYGOD!" came through the wall. Grinning, Mary moved further down his back and away from his sight, knowing he was staring directly at her crotch. "That's good to know Mr. Bliss. I'll be sure to let him know I have your approval."

He grunted an affirmation that Mary hoped meant he'd drop the idea of getting in her pants. Mary for that matter wasn't sure how she felt about the situation. One one side of things, knowing James was screwing another woman. On the other side of things, Mary wasn't so much worried about James wanting that woman, more than he wanted her. It was knowing that right now, his dick was inside someone, and she very much wanted it inside herself. Touching her stomach, she felt that warm flutter inside and smiled at the knowledge, part of him already was.

"Alright Mr. Bliss, I think that's about all we have time for. If you'd like to take a shower, I can lock up when you're done."

He sighed and sat up, before giving her a wink. "Care to join me?"

"No, Mr. Bliss," Mary said, as she turned and thanked that Maggie had agreed he was never coming back.

Henny on the other hand was shaking violently. After that scream, James had insisted on kissing her every time she came. Right now, as her pussy throbbed and spasmed, she physically couldn't lie still through the agonal ecstasy she was feeling as James kept slowly fucking her.

"Please?" she whimpered.

"You want to stop?" James paused.

Henny bit her lip and shook her head, "No, I want you to finish inside me before I have a heart attack."

James grinned. Truth be told, he had been riding the edge since her previous orgasm and was more than ready to find his own release. Leaning in, he captured her lips and held her close. Before thrusting himself firmly inside her. Henny gasped as James firmly thrust up inside her. After the gentle lovemaking they'd shared, his short, hard thrusts had her climbing for an impossible fifth orgasm. She could do little more than moan with each thrust. Until finally, James tightened his grip over her. Henny felt the throb of his cock as he started cumming inside her and she immediately joined him. James held her close as her pussy muscles almost sucked the cum out of him. The sounds she made through their kiss drove him on and he tried his absolute best to keep thrusting right through their combined pleasure. But even as his orgasm came to an end, he pulled away to watch the final moments of Henny's orgasm. Only for her to freeze.

"Again?" He asked.

Her mouth opened as she shuddered bodily and rocked her hips against him one final time. She managed a quick nod of her head, before gasping loudly through one last little death. James just held her close, kissing her softly on the neck and lips between gasping breaths. All too soon she began to relax, before looking up at him with a small smile.

"There now," James smiled. "Are you satisfied?"

"If… If I'm not…"

"Then you come back," James winked. "You come back, and then keep cumming until you are."

Henny sighed and closed her eyes, "I almost wish I wasn't."

James smiled, and pecked her on the lips. Slowly lifting himself, Henny gasped as his cock pulled free from her depths. He looked down at the mess and grinned, seeing him leaking from her.

"Uhg," Henny groaned. "I look gross, don't I?"

James frowned and shook his head, "Not at all. I was thinking how sexy it was seeing me leak out of you."

She blinked, "Really?"

James nodded, "You're a beautiful woman, Henny. You're going to make a wonderful mother. Remember that, okay?"

Henny smiled and nodded, "Okay, and James."

"Yeah?"

She sat up, before leaning in and giving him a small kiss. "Thank you."

With a smile, James patted her bare leg, before standing and dressing quietly. She watched him leave with a heavy heart, before slumping back on the massage table. Touching the mess between her legs she smiled and brought her fingers to her lips for a taste.

James sighed as he stepped into the suite. He came straight back, knowing Maggie and Mary would be waiting for him. And honestly, he just wanted to be with the women he loved. He could hear soft giggling from the room, and he headed in that direction. Coming to a stop in the doorway, he could see Mary's nude form with Maggie between her legs. She was on her back, with her head hanging over the edge, gasping in pleasure as Maggie squatted with their legs entwined. They both rubbed their pussies together and James blinked seeing something purple between them.

"He's watching us," Maggie groaned.

Mary opened her eyes and stared hungrily at him. "You, here, now!"

James thought for a moment, and shook his head. "I… I need a shower."

Mary groaned, "Noooo, we can shower later, I wanna taste."

James blinked, unsure of what to do, when Maggie turned herself around to lay atop Mary. "That's so dirty," she giggled. "I want some too."

With both Maggie and Mary begging, James stepped forward. Mary was the one to undo his pants, while Maggie was the first to take his cock in her mouth. She bobbed her head a few times, while staring up at him. James felt a small tongue caress his balls and groaned as Mary joined in. With a soft gasp, he switched, pulling his cock away from Maggie, who sucked harder so it 'popped' as it came free of her mouth. She gave him a look like she wanted it back, but James paid her no mind as Mary opened her mouth wide. Slipping his cock into her mouth, Mary quickly sucked him down.

"More James," Maggie said, cupping his balls.

"I'll choke her," James frowned.

Mary's hand touched his leg and he pulled away, as she smiled up at him. "Choke me," she grinned.

With a bemused expression, James put his cock back in her mouth. Maggie pulled him closer and James stared, wide eyed as more of his cock pushed into her mouth. When he hit the back of her throat, he tried to pull away, but her hand cupped his ass and pulled him closer.

"She said to choke her," Maggie smiled.

James felt her throat pulse as she swallowed, and pushed the last couple inches into the narrow passage. She made a noise and James suddenly retreated, only for Mary's hand to quickly start stroking him.

"Again," she said, pulling his cock back to her lips.

"Are you sure you want this?" James asked.

Mary lifted his cock from her lips and smiled, "James consent is sexy. Thank you for thinking of me. Right now, what I really want is to feel your cock squirt down my throat."

"That's fucking hot," Maggie groaned as she rocked her hips.

James realised that the dildo or whatever was between them was still in place. So with a last smile at Mary, James angled himself and thrust firmly, but slowly into her throat. He rocked back and forth a few times, before pulling out and letting her breathe. Then he slid back in as she grunted and swallowed to get him deeper. Maggie sat up and James leaned forward to kiss her. As their lips met, he felt Mary prod him so he pulled his cock out of her mouth.

"That's hot," Mary grunted. "Fuck my throat while you kiss her."

Maggie moaned into my mouth as Mary funneled my cock back into her mouth. It became a routine as I fucked her throat for a few moments, then pulled away to let her breath. Then she'd pull him back into her mouth and the cycle would continue.

"You wanna cum, don't you?" Maggie grinned.

James nodded, "This is so hot."

Slipping down, Maggie kissed the bulge in Mary's throat that was James's cock, before kissing her way lower. Mary moaned and twitched under Maggie's kisses and licks. As she got lower, James watched as Maggie took the purple, double-ended dildo and started thrusting it into Mary's pussy. Then with a smile, she leaned down and started tonguing her clit. Almost immediately, Mary tried to cry out. James pulled his cock free of her mouth, but Mary yanked him back in and took him deep, trying to push her own head onto his cock. With a snarl, James found his end and fired the first jet of cum down her throat. Immediately, Mary stopped struggling and just sucked gently as James fed her.

After spending several minutes clustered around Mary, making her the centre of attention. He and Mary then turned to Maggie and left her panting and tired as well. Then they moved into the shower itself. It had been extended and modified so that they could all comfortably fit. James found himself enjoying the closeness of the two women, and made sure to help scrub both their backs. And then as one, they curled up in the large bed. James smiled as Mary and Maggie both used his shoulder as a pillow, and as they drifted off to sleep, he swiftly joined them.

The next day was business as usual. James woke up, Mary

made breakfast while Maggie sucked his dick. James stacked the dishwasher while Mary went down on Maggie at the table. Then James fucked Maggie on his desk after Mary left for her first massage. Everything went to plan, right up until there was a knock on the door. Maggie, who had since cleaned herself up, got up from the temporary station she'd installed and opened the door.

"Hi," Sara mumbled.

"Sara," Maggie smiled, "Come in, what can we do for you?"

The tall woman stepped into the room with slumped shoulders and looked very small. "I… I want to know about your prices."

Maggie paused, "Sara, are you wanting a massage, or a baby?"

She fidgeted nervously for a few moments before sniffing and looking at the floor. "Baby."

"James, how do you feel about this?" Maggie asked, heading for a filing cabinet.

James caught the begging look in Sara's eye and nodded. "I'm fine with it, as long as you and Mary are."

Maggie nodded and took out a small folder. Extracting the paperwork inside, she handed it to Sara. "This is a contract of employment and an NDA. Please go ahead and get a legal representative to check it over, but it is in plain English."

Sara scanned the documents and frowned, "This… This is a ten year work contract, for an unspecified service."

"Pretty much," Maggie nodded. "You get the baby, we get an employee for a decade. Lots of protections in there for the future if you want a raise, or in case of additional expenses and such. In return, if you decide to leave we do a calculation to work out a percentage of the bill to send you depending on how long you worked for us."

"I… Okay," Sara nodded. "Umm, James, do you-"

"Go get it checked," James smiled. "You're in charge of landscaping, however it gets done is your business, you manage your own hours."

"Thank you," she said softly, before stepping out of the room.

"A contract?" James asked.

Maggie shrugged, "It was actually Mary's idea. It's more to do with getting helpful people to stick around. Helpful people that may not be able to afford the service."

"What are we charging for it anyway?

"Minimum, five grand, but it depends on circumstances."

"Five grand?" James frowned. "Should we be charging so much?"

Maggie smiled, "That's what the contracts are for. This is a business. People pay, for you to have sex with them. Now, there's only one of you and there's two women who want more sex with you than anyone else." James smirked and nodded in agreement. "So we've set a price that isn't completely unobtainable, but high enough to stop just anyone coming in. And on the off chance someone like Sara shows up, who's tried and failed for years. Hopefully we can accommodate her."

"Feels almost like blackmail though," James frowned.

"It's not," Maggie smiled and rubbed his shoulder. "The contract is more a gag order than anything. The absolute worst comes to worst, it just means if she voids the contract, we send her the bill for the outstanding amount. There's no punishment or additional clauses to scalp her. There's even a section on payment plans if she can't afford the bill in one lump."

"Do we offer payment plans?"

"Only on the contract. Payment plans would defeat the

purpose of charging at all, the spa is already turning a profit."

James nodded and sighed. "Just, don't let this become everything. I don't want to be some pony getting milked twice a day."

"James," Maggie leaned down and kissed him. "If you're getting milked twice a day, it's once inside me, once inside Mary."

He snorted with laughter, before giving Maggie another kiss. "Alright, what's on for the rest of the day?"

An hour later, the removalists arrived. They were quick and methodical. James stood back while Maggie did her thing, directing the movers into each room as they came available. All the furniture was quickly stripped, before new furniture was brought in. A few remained inside as the others worked, going about assembly and proper placement. James watched as the business that his uncle built, took on new life. There was still work being done on a couple of the cabins, but by now most of it was over. The place felt like it always had. Comfortable, warm, somewhere to relax. It no longer looked like it was a decade out of date either. The furnishings were modern, but comfortable. The lighting was updated and the carpet was new.

Taking a stroll outside, James took in the sight of the place. The lawns were trimmed, the trees pruned and the new drainage channels that Sara had dug were almost invisible. There were children running around one of the play areas they had installed. The building practically gleamed under the light with its fresh coat of paint. As James strolled onward, the sprinklers activated. They were new, something that Sara had put in herself when she decided to create space around each building by building planters and growing everything from flowers, to fruits, vegetables and herbs. Most hadn't made it to maturity yet, but the basil grown up near the restaurant had to be expanded significantly to supply demand.

The roar of an engine caught James's attention. The sound of tires on gravel filled his ears. Turning around, all he could see was a grey sedan, and the face of Mr Bliss careening towards him at speed.

The world lurched and James opened his eyes. The people above him were dressed as paramedics. He thought that was odd as they shined a light into his eyes. Someone was asking him questions, but all he could hear was the voice of two angels, crying out his name. Closing his eyes James rested for a while. When he opened them next, he was inside an ambulance. A familiar hand held his own and he felt the ambulance sway heavily as it took a corner at speed. He squeezed the hand, and heard her gasp, before closing his eyes to rest.

A soft beeping sound roused James from his slumber. The room was dim and someone was sitting beside him, reading a book. James turned his head and waited for his eyes to adjust.

"Baal?"

"This certainly wasn't in the plans," the older man sighed. "How are you feeling?"

James turned his head back to look at the ceiling, "Kinda dizzy."

"That's to be expected," a nurse said, stepping into the room. "Who are you talking to?"

"Ahh," James turned his head to look at Baal, who simply winked. "Nobody, just wondering aloud."

"Alright, well let me take your blood pressure and I'll get someone in here to talk to you."

The nurse did their thing, before quickly leaving, and James was left staring at Baal. "Could have led with that."

The older man smirked, "It was worth the entertainment value at least."

"So what are you doing here anyway?"

"You were in a bad way, if not for me being so close you'd have died," Baal frowned.

James sighed and remembered the expression of hate on Mr Bliss's face as he sped towards him. "I'm guessing I went too far there."

Baal chuckled and shook his head. "No, that was inevitable I believe. She just used your treatment of her as the final straw to make the decision."

"And Henny?"

"She's fine," Baal sighed. "A little bruised and battered after being thrown from the vehicle-"

"What!?"

"Shhh!" Baal held out a hand. "This is all the details of the curse. That's why I'm here. There's nothing in this if you and her die. You nearly did, she was mostly fine, that's why I'm here with you. The doctors are still scratching their heads about you. They brought you in for…"

"Mr Kirk?" A woman called, knocking on the door.

"Yes?"

"Oh good, I wasn't sure what to expect. Not after… Anyway," she smiled. "I'm doctor Grace, I've been informed of your… Situation. The good news is, it appears to be a concussion. The bad thing is you have several cracked ribs and some bruising. We've done what we can, but there's little else other than pain management. Do you have anyone that can pick you up in the morning?"

"Yeah, I'll have it sorted."

"Great!"

With an awkward nod, the woman left.

James turned to Baal, "So you were saying?"

"You died," Baal said with a shrug. "The paramedics were able to revive you, once you were alive again, I did what I could to put you back together. Maggie rode with you in the ambulance to the hospital and by the time we got back, what they thought was massive internal bleeding and shattered bones, turned into a much easier situation to deal with."

"Oh," James frowned. "Thank you."

Baal shrugged, "It's the rules of the curse. I need you to be in good health to perform."

James snorted before grimacing at the sudden ache in his chest. "Oh fuck, that's not going to make things easy."

"Reverse cowgirl is still an option if the ladies are careful."

This time James had to grit his teeth to stop him from laughing loudly.

CHAPTER EIGHT

James sighed as he stared at the television. It had barely been used the whole time he had been living there. Now, two days after coming home from the hospital, it was his lifeline. He wasn't really watching it though, as he reflected on the previous days' events. The police had taken his statement. James had explained that after providing his service to Henrietta, she and her husband had left. When the police asked about the service he provided, James told them he offered a homeo-pathic fertility treatment.

The police put two and two together, collected the video camera footage of Mr. Bliss running James down, and promptly left. James was then given very specific orders to remain seated and do as little as possible. Which was fine, right up until Mary and Maggie both left to work. So James found himself truly alone, for the first time in weeks, staring at the idiot box. With a sigh, James's stomach rumbled and he glanced at the refrigerator. He patted his pocket for his phone, before sighing as he remembered it was broken. The phone was crushed by the impact of the car and tossed into the wet grass as he tumbled across the ground.

Before he could decide if it was going to be worth getting up, the door softly opened to admit a food cart.

"Ummm, I have lunch, sir," Henny said in a small voice.

James just gaped at her for a few moments as she came in. He could see the swelling over her eye and a similar looking gravel rash that he had on his arms. When she lifted her gaze to look at him, and saw him staring back, she froze.

"I-I'm sorry," she murmured.

She turned on the spot and made it as far as the door before a hand caught her by the wrist. She thought about the feeling of her soon-to-be ex-husband striking her and she closed her eyes as she was pulled around. It was the soft hug that caught her instead. James grit his teeth in pain, his ribs still hurt a lot, but he was so very relieved to see Henny was okay. Leaning back, he cupped her face and without a second thought, he kissed her softly. Henny's reaction was immediate. Letting out a small sob, she leaned into James, only to feel him flinch. All at once she remembered his injuries and sprung out of his arms.

"You need to be resting!" She cried as tears kept rolling down her cheeks.

James looked at her and smiled, despite the pain he was in. Keeping hold of her hand, he turned and led her back to the couch. Henny felt herself being guided down to sit by the young man, but it was only as he frowned at her bruising, she realised who he was.

"Sir-"

"James," he corrected.

"James, I'm so so-"

"You don't apologise for him," James cut her off again. "It wasn't your actions that hit you, threw you out of a moving car and ran me over."

"I-I…" She stammered for a bit, lost in what she wanted to say. The soft smile he directed her way, made her mind go blank, as she remembered the softness of his lips. Looking around for something to pull her attention, her eyes landed on the cart. "Lunch!" She squeaked.

Before James could respond, she was up again. Plucking the tray from the cart, James could see it was one of those self standing ones. Henny flicked out the legs and sat the tray so it was perched over his lap. She stood, flashed him a professional smile and reached for the cart.

"Please wait?" He asked softly.

Henny froze in indecision. With a quivering lip, she turned back to him and fought through the smile. "Yes s- James?"

"I'm assuming the ladies are responsible for you being here?"

"Yes James," she repeated.

James nodded for a moment, "Are you happy?"

The question threw her off. She froze for a moment and wondered quite what he meant. The sincere look in his eye left little to the imagination. "Yes… I'm helping run the kitchen, in return for a place to stay."

"Wages?"

"They're being held, until I can get a bank account of my own," Henny said softly.

"If you need anything, just ask, and I'll get you cash in the meantime, okay?"

She smiled for a moment and nodded, before wiping the tears from her face, carefully to avoid her swelling. "Thank you," she said.

James watched her leave with a sad smile. He was glad to know she was okay, and admittedly a little confused that she was still here. When he thought about it, he was actually quite relieved she hadn't been badly hurt. That or taken it upon herself to vanish entirely. He knew getting attached to clients wasn't a good idea, but… Henny was something special.

With a sigh, James lifted off the warming lid and smiled at the sandwich he was provided with. Turkish bread with salad, a chutney of some kind and a piece of steak smothered in melted cheese. He drooled just thinking about it as he picked up the steak knife and started cutting. He'd separated the sandwich into three parts when the door opened again.

"Oh, Henny didn't stay?" Mary asked, coming in.

James shook his head, "No, she seemed a bit emotional…" He thought back on his reaction when he first saw her. "I kissed her."

"You kissed her?" Mary asked.

Nodding, James sighed. "Yes, I'm sorry, I was just so relieved to see she was okay and I didn't even think."

"Dammit," Mary grunted.

James nodded, knowing what was about to happen, right up until Mary pulled off her shirt. "What, ah…"

"Put the tray aside and grab a piece of that sandwich," Mary grumbled.

"What's going on?" James asked as Mary reached up behind and unclipped her bra. As it joined her shirt on the floor, his eyes locked on her swaying breasts.

"I made a stupid bet," Mary grumbled, getting to her knees and pushing his legs apart. "C'mon, I'm on my lunch break, I need to be quick."

"Right," James frowned, still clearly confused.

Leaning back, he watched Mary rub her breasts with her hands. He was rock hard as she smiled up at him. Plucking a piece of sandwich, Mary grinned and reached for his fly. James groaned as he bit into the sandwich and tasted the combination of flavours. The sweetness of the chutney was balanced by the sharpness of the cheese. The crisp, fresh salad dulled the smoke and salt from the steak, while the fresh bread rounded off the flavour. He moaned a second time as his cock sprung into the air, and a third as Mary sunk her mouth over it.

James was on edge, he'd gone from multiple orgasms a day between both ladies, to nothing while he recovered. They collectively decided that it wasn't safe to get him riled up, and he was confined to listening to them go down on one another in the shower. It was an exquisite form of torture, that Mary was making up for as she swirled her tongue over the head of his cock.

"Oh fuck," James grunted.

Mary just moaned in appreciation as his seed fired into her mouth. She bobbed her head softly and kept up the suction as James blissed out where he sat. With a small pop, Mary pulled her head away and shot him a quick smile.

"What was that about?" James asked.

"Mmm," Mary shook her head as she threw on her shirt without the bra.

James watched in confusion as she quickly left the suite. Clearly he was missing something, but if Mary was blowing him, it probably wasn't a bad thing. Eating the rest of his sandwich, it was only when the door opened yet again, he realised his dick was still hanging out. Reaching for it, he froze, seeing Mary's predatory gaze as she stalked back into the room.

"That bitch!" she snapped.

James frowned, "What happened?"

Mary shuddered and rubbed her thighs for a moment. "She made me spit it inside her."

"What?" James asked in monotone.

Mary grimaced and got on her knees again, "We had a bet, about how you'd react to Henny. I thought you'd take charge and fuck her, Maggie thought you'd be sweet and kiss her. We haven't touched you in days, so I thought it was a safe bet. I lost, so I had to blow you and bring your load to her."

"And…"

"And she got up on your desk, pulled her panties aside and told me where I had to put it."

James grew suddenly erect at the thought. His breath hitched for a moment while he tried to rein himself in, but he didn't make it very far before Mary was blowing him for the second time. Grunting in appreciation, James laid back as Mary's mouth popped free. He opened his eyes as she slid her pants down, before reaching for her panties.

"Leave em on," James requested.

Mary paused, before smiling and climbing onto the couch. With her legs either side of his own, she leaned in and kissed him. James gently ran his hands up her sides, making her moan into the kiss. When he found her breasts, her nipples were hard little points that pressed into his palms. Keeping one hand on her breasts, the other went between her legs and James grinned as he felt the dampness soaking into her panties.

"You're a bad man," she whispered as she pulled away. Reaching down between them, she slapped his hand away. With one finger, she dug under the elastic and pulled her panties to one side, giving James a perfect view of a string of grool that curved from her pussy to her knuckle. "Tell me if I do something that hurts, I need this so bad."

James sighed as her firm grip tilted his cock into position, before she lowered herself onto him. The wide, delicious grin on her face as she impaled herself made James smile.

"It's already happening, isn't it?" James asked as Mary began to lift herself.

"What's happening?" She asked with her eyes closed.

James reached up and palmed both her breasts and he

imagined they were heavier than he was used to. "You, turning into a horny, pregnant slut, desperate for my-"

"Yes!" She trembled and forced herself to the balls in a single drop of her hips. "Yes, I'm a horny pregnant slut," she whimpered, raising and lowering herself. "All I've thought about for two days, is the feeling of you cumming inside me."

"Fuck," James grunted. He ignored the mild throb of his ribs as Mary bounced on the length of his cock. His eyes were fixed on the sight of her labia as they caressed his length with every upstroke. "You're really loving this, aren't you?"

"Yes," Mary grunted. "I know it messes with a lot of women, but being pregnant feels amazing right now."

James grinned as she continued to bounce on his lap, "Are you going to cum for me?"

She beamed widely and nodded, "Uh huh."

James watched her eyes tighten as her legs began to twitch, "If you're going to be this sexy every time you're pregnant. You're going to be pregnant for a very long time, you know that?"

All he heard was the soft gasp of her voice, before her pussy tightened down on his cock. The rhythmic pulsing of her pussy was heavenly, but James wasn't ready after his earlier blowjob. Gripping her hips, he knew he couldn't lift or bounce her, in his condition. So he dragged her hips back and forth instead.

"James!" Mary squealed as her eyes went wide.

"That's right," James grinned as he forced her hips back, dragging her clit across his pubic bone. "Pregnant sluts get to cum on my dick until I say otherwise."

Mary gasped loudly and leaned forward. Immediately James felt her tongue invade his mouth. Matching her efforts, Mary started thrusting her hips back and forth with the same movement he was dragging her. So instead he put his arms around her. Mary hissed and squealed softly into his mouth, unwilling to pull away as she delved into the sensation running between her legs. When she felt him tense beneath her, it was only a few moments before she felt him throb up inside her. Concentrating on that feeling, she rose quickly to her own end, before crying out softly into his mouth. James just kept kissing her as her pussy started to clench and pulse once again. As the final spurts of his cum fired up inside her, her pussy milked them away hungrily. He didn't have to worry about overstimulation as she softly shuddered and moaned above him, leaving James to kiss the woman he loved and enjoy the contact they had.

When she finally pulled away, she smiled dreamily at him.

"Mary!" Maggie snapped. "Get off him, now!"

Mary shot James a sly grin as she slipped back and off his cock. James pouted as her labia released him from their embrace. But it was Maggie who shocked them both. Mary froze as she felt hands pull her ass cheeks apart and she squeaked as she felt a tongue lick from clit to ass, collecting all of James's leaked seed. She stood, before bringing her hand down on Mary's ass for a firm slap as she swallowed the offering she'd taken.

"Get that ass in the shower or so help me god!"

Mary shot James another grin, before skipping off to the shower. That left him with Maggie who glared at him as well. "I know you're injured, so I'm not going to give you the spanking SHE deserves. But I do need to punish you."

Before James could question it, Maggie was between his legs, licking and gently kissing his cock. Despite having finished twice, he slowly rose for the third time as Maggie slurped on the tip. She gripped the base of his cock firmly and made a twisting motion at the same time, leaving James gasping in bliss. And right when he felt himself getting to that point, she pulled away and stood.

"What?" James grunted.

"You shouldn't be encouraging her, she could have injured you!" Maggie snapped.

James glanced at his cock, then at Maggie, then back at his cock, "You're the one with the stupid bet!"

At that, Maggie blushed and seemed to stumble on what to say next.

"Fuck him, or blow him!" Mary yelled from the hallway.

James grit his teeth in discomfort, "If you blue ball me, when I'm better, I'm going to tie you to a massage table, and do horrible things to you."

Maggie trembled for a few moments as she remembered the thought that ran through her mind when they first had sex all those weeks ago. "I'll make you a deal," she said as James glared at her. The look in his eye had a dangerous edge, but she wasn't scared, merely... Excited. "If you promise to tie me to a massage table and do horrible things to me, I'll make sure someone sucks your dick at least three times a day."

"Deal," James grunted.

Immediately, Maggie dropped to her knees and took his cock between her lips. James grunted at the sudden sensation. Without thinking, he gripped the back of her head, but that only spurred her on as she forced herself further down. She didn't have the same depth control as Mary did, and made a small noise. Before he could try and pull her away, she did herself. With her mouth open and her tongue rolling out, there was a line of saliva connecting the eye of his cock to the tip of her tongue. She looked James in the eye and held his gaze as she lowered her lips once again.

With his hands loosely holding her hair, and Maggie's eyes locked on his, James watched Maggie turn into a sex goddess as she slowly mouthed his erection. Despite how slowly she moved, she bathed his cock with her tongue and moaned in appreciation until he came uncontrollably in her mouth. Maggie moaned in delight as she suckled at the head. Third time round, James was actually relieved she didn't do anything more as he was sensitive enough. As Maggie pulled away, still keeping eye contact, and swallowed… James had to fight the urge to test his limits. This time, as the two ladies went back to work, James decided it was worth having a small nap.

James awoke alone the following day. He sighed, missing the presence of his two pregnant loves. They had been reluctant to use his shoulders as pillows as they had in the past, on account of his ribs. So despite knowing that Maggie was meeting with a surveyor, while Mary had an early morning client, he still felt rather put out by waking alone.

With a grunt and a groan, he sat himself up and swung his legs over the side of the bed. Hoisting himself to his feet, James made the slow walk into the bathroom. After quickly relieving himself, he hopped in the shower until he felt vaguely human. With a sigh, James hopped out and dried himself off, noting his pain had significantly decreased.

"Need to talk to Baal," he muttered softly to himself.

Hanging up his towel, James stepped out of the bathroom and jumped at the sound of a metallic crash. Whirling around, Henny stood at the end of the hall with another food cart. She had been in the process of setting up what looked like bacon and eggs, when he'd come out and she'd dropped one of the covers.

"Henny!" James gasped, before realising he was completely naked.

Clearly that was why she had dropped the cover, as she blushed fiercely. "I-I was bringing b-breakfast."

James nodded, "Right, I'll-"

"In bed," Henny added.

James just nodded and headed for the room. He could

hear her coming up behind him, so he didn't bother pausing to put anything on, before climbing into the bed. Pulling the blanket up to his waist, James got comfortable. Henny lifted the same tray as lunch the day before. With practiced ease, she flicked out the supports and set the table over his waist. James smiled at the perfect looking meal, before glancing up at Henny, who looked extremely nervous.

"Are you okay?"

She nodded as she wrung her hands together, "I want this," she said softly.

Before dropping to her knees. James froze as she placed one hand on the tray, and the other on his blanket. As she pulled it free, exposing his semi-rigid cock, James found his voice.

"What are you doing?"

Henny blinked, before looking uncertain. "M-Maggie… She asked me to…" Henyy trailed off nervously

James blinked and sighed internally. This is what Maggie meant when SOMEONE sucks his dick three times a day. "Okay," James said softly. "I'm not going to press either way, I'm just happy to see you."

Henny blinked slowly, before smiling. She reached up and took hold of James's cock and gave it a couple strokes. It firmed in her hand and she dived over the top. James grunted as he spooned a mouthful of egg into his mouth. Henny wasn't as skilled as Maggie or Mary, but her enthusiasm caught him by surprise. He felt himself surge to full mast as she took half his cock into her mouth. He watched her tuck her hair behind her ear, before taking hold of his base with one hand. The slight grate of teeth made him hiss, and she immediately came to a stop, staring up at him.

James swallowed his mouthful and smiled softly. "Teeth," he said gently.Hennyy frowned for a moment, before very lightly biting. James grinned and shook his head, "No no.

Teeth bad. What you're doing with your head and hand is lovely. But more tongue and a little more suction would be great."

Henny seemed to ponder for a moment, before running her tongue over the sensitive underside of his cock. Immediately James shuddered and let out a soft groan. That set her off and she started bobbing her head. Each downstroke went right to the back of her mouth, stopping before she choked. On the upstroke, she dragged her entire tongue up his length and over the head. James just shuddered and closed his eyes as he enjoyed the sensation. But Henny released his cock with a huff.

"Young man, you will eat your breakfast!" She snapped in the tone of voice she'd used when they first met.

James smirked and opened his eyes. Looking at the serious expression on her face, James picked up his fork and transferred a piece of bacon into his mouth. As he bit down and moaned through the flavour, Henny pushed his cock past her lips, making him moan twice. It then became a game, where Henny watched as he ate. While he chewed, she lightly bobbed her head, inching him closer to his release. When he scooped up another mouthful, she pulled her mouth right to the tip, and as he took that first bite, she forced herself right down again. For all her inexperience, James was trembling and trying to stay rational by the end of the meal.

Dropping his fork back on the plate, he sighed, "That was delicious."

Henny made a cute purring noise, before pushing her head down over his cock. James tensed as she very vigorously sucked his entire length in and out of her mouth. He felt his orgasm rapidly approaching and grit his teeth. He remembered the facial he gave her last time and didn't know how she was going to react.

"Henny! Henny, I'm going to cum!"

She let out a delighted noise, but didn't pull his cock out or slow. Instead she cupped his balls with his other hand and James gave a last shudder.

"Cumming!" He grunted.

All at once, he unleashed in Henny's mouth. She made a squeal and backed off, so only the head of his cock was in her mouth. She licked at the underside of the head as he came directly over her tongue. The hand that held the base of his cock stroked gently back and forth, while her hand cupped his balls and lightly fondled. As Henny sucked the last spurt of his cum into her mouth, she sealed her lips against him and drew away. Sitting upright, she saw the satisfied look in his eyes.

James watched as Henny opened her mouth, showing him the white mess, pooled over her tongue. She closed her mouth and visibly swallowed, making James shiver. Henny smiled, before leaning forward and lightly kissing his cock, before standing and removing the tray. As she replaced it on the cart, she turned and headed for the door, when James cleared his throat.

"Henny, please don't do anything you don't want to, okay?"

Henny turned her head and blushed as she nodded, "I wanted to."

James nodded and Henny started moving again. Glancing down at his cock, James groaned, seeing himself stand back to attention. Rubbing his face, James made a quick plan of action, before sarcastically smirking, "Thanks Baal."

Maggie was on her hands and knees, digging through the bottom drawer looking for her documents on the land they'd bought. She'd just gotten an email stating the area was being listed as a national park, so that meant any small pockets of land between the spa, and the park would probably drop in value. If that were the case, there might be a good deal involved.

It was as she straightened, the door opened behind her. Her immediate thought was that only Mary would come in without knocking. So when the folder was pulled from her hands, Maggie jumped in shock, before settling her eyes on James. In a flash, his lips were on hers. Maggie moaned in appreciation, before trying to pry him off.

"James, you're hurt!" She got out as he moved to kiss the side of her neck.

"I'm horny," he replied, undoing the button on her slacks.

"Didn't Henny take care of you?" She gasped as he slipped his hands around to cup her ass.

"Yup, and now it's your turn," he growled softly.

Maggie trembled as he removed his hands. James firmly guided her around and gave her a quick shove so she bumped up against his desk. Without thinking, she leaned over and gripped the edges of the desk. Which was the perfect angle for James to quickly pull her pants down with her panties. James watched the thin line of grool stretch from her labia to a spot on the pink lace in his hand. He only pushed it down to mid thigh, something about the contrast from Maggie's pale ass, to the pink panties, to her black slacks made him hungry.

"James, seriously, you shouldn't be doing this, you need to be resting," she hissed at him.

"Do you want me to stop?" He asked, midway through unzipping his fly.

"...No-"

"Then quiet," James slapped her ass, enjoying the small jiggle it made. "I'm fucking you."

"Mmmm," Maggie moaned as she felt his hands pry her ass cheeks apart.

But it was the tongue that slid into her pussy that made

her gasp. James forced the muscle as deep inside her as he could reach. Even as aroused as she already was, foreplay had its uses. Maggie made soft noises of appreciation as he rolled his tongue inside her. With his face pressed right into her silken folds, James reached up between them and wet his thumb with her juices. Moving higher, James stroked her clit and smirked into her dripping pussy as Maggie began to squirm.

She could feel that ball of heat building inside her as he stroked her Clit. Maggie's breath came in short, sharp bursts. The stroking on her clit was an exquisite torture. Enough stimulation to bring her to the brink, but not enough to push her over the edge. She was contemplating begging when his tongue pulled out of her, running up and over her small asshole. It made her shudder at the contact, before she lifted her head to see why he stopped. As she did so, a firm hand pressed her all the way down onto the desk. She could see out of the corner of her eye, the stamp of approval for the sale. It was meaningless beside the feeling of James's cock stretching her open. The door suddenly opened, and Maggie had only the barest notion to look. Not that it mattered in her blissed out state, but she was somewhat relieved to see it was Mary.

"You, here, now!" James growled.

Mary shuffled over as James started thrusting his cock in and out of Maggie. The expression on her face was obvious and Mary blushed when she realised it was affecting her as well. "James, you really should-"

"Nope, get your pants off," James snapped.

Mary blinked in surprise, before smiling widely. Undoing her top button, she wiggled her hips seductively as she began pushing them down. "What brought this on?"

"It's been three days since I've been able to do this. I'm already inside Maggie," he gave her ass a slap, making her jump and kick her legs uselessly. "So play with yourself for me so I can fuck you as well."

Mary glanced down at Maggie, who was drooling a little and slipped her hand between her legs. She surprised herself when her labia were already slick and she hissed at the sensation of her fingers gliding through them. Leaning on the desk, she barely paid attention to James as she circled her own clit with her fingers. Reaching down with two hands, she kept up the pressure, while slipping fingers into herself.

"Stop!" James growled.

Mary's attention snapped back to him and she frowned, right up until he grabbed her. Maggie let out a small grunt of disappointment as James pulled his cock out of her. She let out a small squeak as James shoved Mary on top of her. With Maggie and Mary stacked on one another, James pushed his cock into Mary. She let out a few gasps and wriggled into a more comfortable position. Mary's wriggling pushed Maggie's hips into the edge of the desk, where each thrust into her friend caused her clit to rub. She grit her teeth as that pressure built up to breaking point. Right as James slammed his cock back inside her.

"Oh fuck!" Maggie cried.

James grit his teeth as he felt Mary's pussy clench over him. He shortened his thrusts, but kept them up. She gasped and writhed with each one, so he knew it was driving her crazy. Yanking himself free of Maggie, James pushed himself straight back into Mary. She on the other hand arched her back, pushing her hips down. She angled herself so his cock would drive against her front wall and it worked perfectly. But it also increased the pressure on Maggie's hips, forcing her clit harder into the corner of the desk. Her fingernails scraped the polished wood, unable to escape or cling to anything in an effort to distract herself. So she was forced to feel the full, undiluted effects of the pressure on her clit.

Mary began to shudder as James's cock rubbed over her g-spot with each thrust. She gasped silently at the ceiling as her pussy spasmed uncontrollably as James thrust up inside her. The sensation began to get too much and Mary lifted herself off. James was still lucid enough to get the hint, but he wasn't quite finished. Seeing as Mary had had enough for the time being, he pushed his cock back inside Maggie, who squealed into the table. Making a few thrusts, he grit his teeth as she immediately hit her second orgasm, and James slammed his cock to the base as he emptied himself inside her at the same time.

Gasping at the intensity of her cumming over his dick, James finally slumped back, pulling his cock free. Mary was mostly upright, panting, with a large smile on her face. Now she had the room, she slid off Maggie and stretched. As she looked down at the mess James left, Mary leaned down to help clean it up.

And as Maggie's soft squeals filled the office once more, James grinned as he watched Mary's ass sway before him as she enjoyed her meal.

CHAPTER NINE

After a day of James relieving his frustrations, Maggie had agreed it was safe for him to return to work. Not that it meant much going from being confined to his suite, to being confined to his office. Which is how James knew they were in trouble.

"Spill," Maggie sighed from beside him.

The office was large enough that instead of Maggie organising a restructure, she had James's desk replaced and she sat on the opposite side. It was a little tight, but James felt good about keeping her close.

"There's so much," James grumbled, reading a report on their finances.

"No more than usual," Maggie replied.

James nodded in agreement, "But that is changing. Things are picking up already and after taking a few days off I'm already swamped. Half of what I'm doing is working out whether it's a legal thing, or a financial thing and I STILL managed to send you a report you'd just sent me."

"Sounds like you need an assistant," Maggie offered.

James paused, before looking at her. He saw the smirk

and shook his head. "I'm not hiring an assistant just so I can bang her."

"I didn't even say HER," Maggie giggled.

James groaned and shook his head, "Either way, can you put out an ad for an assistant?"

"James honey?"

He looked up and saw her blink sexily at him, "Ummm, yeah?"

"No matter how many times you bend me over this desk and make me squeal your name, I'm NOT your assistant."

James blinked, wondering if that was both an instruction to make the ad himself, AND screw her, or if he was going to have to screw her later. In any case, he was saved from having to come to that decision, by a knock on the door.

"Come in!" Maggie called.

The door opened as Baal stepped into the room. He shot Maggie a smile, earning on in return before he turned his attention to me.

"James, how are you feeling?"

"I'm good, I suppose my rapid advance in condition over the last few days is because of you?"

Baal took a deep breath, before nodding, "Six months."

"What?-"

"Oh god," Maggie gasped.

James looked from Baal, to Maggie and saw her eyes snap to him. In her expression was fear. And it dawned on him what that meant.

"My lifespan, recovering from that, took six months of my life?"

Baal nodded slowly. "The energy came from somewhere. I deal in lifeforce, so I took what I had to, to keep you alive."

Maggie jumped to her feet, "I'm getting Sara."

James watched her storm from the room, while Baal smiled reassuringly. "I want you to understand the level of risk involved. The human body is relatively easy to keep from breaking down. That's what part of the energy is used for, but actively keeping it alive is a whole other thing. Especially when you've been hit by a car."

"That's hardly my fault," James sighed.

"I know," Baal nodded. "That's why I called it a curse. It isn't fair and the rules are absolute. Either you will have lots of children, or you will die."

As the older man turned and grabbed the door handle, James sighed. "Thank you Baal."

"You're welcome"

James smiled thinking of Maggie, Mary and indeed Henny. When Baal stepped out of the room, the door didn't swing quite closed before Maggie burst back in.

"You, suite, now."

"Maggie-"

"Now!" she snapped, before a tear rolled down her cheek.

James got up and moved around the desk, before pulling her gently into his arms. She shuddered for a moment, before straightening up and pulling away.

"I love you," James said, kissing her softly.

Maggie smiled as his lips broke away, but a tear still escaped the corner of her eye. "Six months, James. You're not getting that back. Mary, Henny, even Sara and I. We're not young women."

"Please don't," James cringed.

"You need to be there for our children," Maggie kissed him softly. "There's going to be lots of them. Family reunions will be a nightmare, I'm sure. But of all of us, you're the one who will probably be here the longest."

"I don't like thinking about that," James grumbled.

Maggie let out a small chuckle, "Then don't. Just go back to the suite, and pump a baby into Sara. And once she's good and pregnant, you come out and advertise for a new assistant, while I find some more clients… Please?"

"Fine," James sighed. "On one condition?"

Maggie blinked for a moment, "Let me hear it."

James grinned as he stepped out of his office. He was thoroughly looking forward to dessert. And after texting Mary to get her on board, James was ready to spend a little time with Sara. Stepping into the room, he could hear the shower running.

"It's just me!" James called, kicking off his shoes.

"Oh good!" Sara called out. "You can do my back for me!"

With a grin, James remembered how she'd taken charge that day. She was a woman that knew what she wanted and he wasn't one to question her. Striding into the bathroom, James watched the silhouette of Sara through the mist covered glass. She seemed to be washing her hair.

"You coming in?" She called.

James grinned and stripped off his clothes and after dropping them in the hamper, he pulled the door open. Sara stood there, tall, proud and extremely naked. Broad shoulders supported large, well rounded breasts. Her stomach, hips and legs all showed considerable definition, right down to her pink toenails. Looking back up, Sara was stroking the water from her long brown hair, while looking rather self conscious.

"You are absolutely beautiful," James said with complete honesty.

The big woman snorted and turned away with a smile. "Come on then, this back isn't going to scrub itself."

James knew she was trying to hide how relieved she was that he hadn't turned her down. In truth, he marvelled at her. He'd seen many women of many shapes and sizes, but he'd never been with a woman that could quite literally bench press him. Reaching over, James grabbed the soap and a loofah. Then he started scrubbing. When his hands touched her flesh, James felt the muscles in her back. He admired how they moved and how they responded to his touch. He made sure to be firm enough to give a gentle massage, but gentle enough not to cause discomfort. In order to reach the tops of her shoulders, James had to press up close, and Sara flinched as his not erect cock, slid across her ass.

"I'm going to rinse off," she said softly.

James nodded and stepped back, as Sara moved under the stream of water. As he watched, he missed the gleam in her eye as she snatched the soap and started applying it to him. One look at her, and James kept his mouth shut as Sara rubbed him down. Turning him, she pressed James into the wall, as she stroked his soapy cock with one hand.

"It only takes one time, right?"

"Yeah," James grunted through the sensation of her hand on his dick.

"Then you're going to forgive me for taking my time. It's been years since something with a heartbeat has been inside me."

When her hand released him, James groaned, but Sara just sprayed him quickly with water and got on her knees. He didn't have any response as she took his cock in her mouth. The look she gave was almost predatory. James had no questions about who was in charge this time. He shuddered as her tongue lapped at the sensitive underside of his cock. Sara wasted no time and was taking no prisoners. James had little more options than to gasp and start cumming directly into her mouth. As his seed touched her tongue, Sara made a delighted noise and slowly massaged the head with her tongue. James was left panting and trembling as Sara sucked him dry. And with a small kiss on the end of his cock, Sara stood and smiled down on the younger man.

"You okay?" She asked with a smirk.

James nodded for a moment, before shifting beneath the water stream. It only took a moment to rinse himself, before he followed Sara out of the shower. James grabbed his towel, before taking a spare out for Sara, which she took with a grateful smile. He had a brief idea of toweling her dry, but wasn't sure if she'd be comfortable with it. In the end though, the situation quickly spiraled as she grabbed his hand and yanked him from the bathroom. James found himself being gently deposited on the bed by the aggressive woman, and as she climbed on top of him, he couldn't help but smirk.

"What?" She grumbled, massaging him back to full mast.

James grinned as he enjoyed the feeling of her hands. "Just remembering last time you had me in this position."

Sara blushed and nodded, "You got me so hot and bothered, I didn't know what to do with myself."

"Now you do," James grinned.

Sara seemed to feel how hard James was for a moment, before tilting her head. "James, don't bullshit me, alright. Cos I'm going to fuck you, this is happening, you're going in me. But do you REALLY have a magic penis?"

"Yes," James said slowly. "If you get on my cock, you will fall pregnant."

"I just," Sara raised herself up and fit James's cock to her entrance. "How do I know, I'll be a good mommy?"

The feeling of her pussy spreading over his cock, made James sigh in pleasure. "You're beautiful, smart and driven," James grunted as Sara raised and lowered herself on his cock. "If you think you're doing something wrong, you'll fix it." Sara smiled and nodded as she added a rocking motion to her hips. "And... If you're staying on, and you don't mind... I could..."

Sara slowed and came to a stop with James buried to the hilt inside her. "Are you offering to stay in my life, so my child will have a father?"

"If you want, yes."

James moaned into the kiss as Sara slammed down on top of him. He was completely engulfed by the larger woman, not that he cared a lick. She thrust her hips back and forth, moaning into James's mouth as she fucked him. James did his best to rock his own hips, driving himself up into her clit with each stroke. Sara had always enjoyed sex, but this felt different. She didn't know if it was just having a new lover, or the hope of a pregnancy over the top. As James's grip tightened around her, she realised he was cumming. She felt something leaking out of her with each thrust and slammed into her own orgasm.

James was practically gasping. Sara's hard, fast strokes were incredibly intense. They had quickly driven him to the point, before shoving him over. As he erupted inside her, James held on to the larger woman, hoping she'd slow down. Instead, her pussy clenched around his cock and James was left trapped in a perpetual state of pleasure. Each pulse of his cock was met by the firm squeeze of Sara's muscular contractions. Each of those contractions was accompanied by a short, hard thrust of her hips, that drove him into the deepest point possible inside her.

ALICE SIGHED as she nodded politely in Donna's office. She regretted thinking of him like it, but James made an excellent buffer. The young man used to make her smile. He was quiet, polite and didn't spend anywhere near as much time staring at her tits as some of her other coworkers. And now he was gone, she was stuck facing the brunt of Donna's wrath.

"I tell you, that idiot didn't know a SINGLE THING about running a business!" Donna snapped. "I mean look at it, this is all gibberish!"

Alice leaned around the desk and saw the screen. She frowned for a moment at what she was seeing. "Donna, you've used the wrong program."

"Don't you start!" Donna rounded on her instead. "This is the same program I always use, and it's always worked before!"

Alice watched in horror as Donna started deleting sections of the file. It wasn't programming per se, but what Donna had opened was the contents of the report, rather than the report itself. It should have been a simple word document, but she'd opened it in a different program. Alice watched in horror as Donna deleted anything that wasn't strictly related to the report, including all the markers for formatting, font and other things.

"There," Donna snapped, hitting save and closing. "Now to print."

Alice watched in horror as Donna now tried to open the document with the correct program, only for it to immediately crash.

"Oh now what?" Donna growled.

"Donna-"

"I need you to ring IT for me. I need this report fixed today. I can't believe he managed to fuck this up!"

Donna sighed, "I'll get right on it."

Getting to her feet, she let herself out of Donna's office, before hanging her head.

"You okay?" One of the older ladies on the floor asked.

Alice nodded slowly, before glancing over. Ella was a wonderful, kind woman. Her entire desk was covered in photographs of her kids and grandkids. Her husband had passed on a few years back, but she'd stuck around apparently out of boredom.

"I think I need a holiday," Alice sighed.

Ella nodded for a moment, "Any plans this weekend?"

"Nope," Alice laughed in a self-deprecating way. "No, I haven't had weekend plans since before James left."

Ella grinned, "He was always a bit sweet on you."

Alice shrugged, "Doesn't matter now though, does it?"

"Tell you what, I have a gift voucher for a spa weekend I've been meaning to use."

"I can't take that from you," Ella smiled.

"It's for a couples suite," Ella smiled. "We can go as friends, though we'll have to share a room. I promise I don't snore. But we can get massages, take a walk in the bush, they even do movie nights with pizza!"

Alice looked at the hopeful smile on Ella's face, and realised the older woman was probably as lonely as she was. "Fine, but no making fun of my pink jammies!"

Ella's face broke into a delighted smile, "I'll bring my purple ones! Who knows, maybe there's a sexy masseuse who will sweep you off your feet!"

Alice snorted as she tried not to laugh, but Ella had no such compunction. When Alice got back to her desk, she quickly looked up the name of the spa and quickly went through their services. She liked the look and the prices of everything seemed reasonable. It was also only a few hours drive away. Scrolling through the last of the site, she was sold and happy to be tagging along with Ella. Even if this facility did have one ridiculous service.

"Pregnancy guaranteed, pffft," Alice rolled her eyes. "Probably a gimmick to get the old ladies in."

"What's a gimmick?" Donna snapped, coming around the corner.

"Oh," Alice froze and closed the screen, "Just IT's wait times. Their system said to give them five minutes and try again."

"Useless," Donna spat. "Whole company is run by idiots."

Alice watched Donna stalk away and rolled her eyes.

"Wonder if that fertility treatment has a happy ending," she giggled.

JAMES HAD GOTTEN the text twenty minutes ago and was still eating. Which was the plan he'd set in place with Mary. James chewed the last piece of steak, savoring the flavours of the fats, salts and the pepper that brought it so simply together. In any case, after a long day of hard work.. Pun intended. He was up for a little more hard work. Standing, James packed away his dish, before returning it to the kitchen.

"All done?" Henny asked.

"It was wonderful," James smiled. "Just what I needed after today. Thank you."

Henny smiled and wandered off, so James made his way back to the suite. He was going to take his time. Twenty minutes later, James was showered and dressed in a shirt and slacks. He was comfortable and ready for his evening. So he strode from the suite and made for the massage rooms. They always used the same room, so it was no hassle to find the one with the 'Do Not Disturb' card on the door handle.

Turning the door handle, James stepped into the room to see his prize, and froze. Maggie was staring at him with wide open eyes. He could just see the edges of some lace poking out from around the tape covering her mouth. Which told him where her panties most likely were. Maggie was completely naked, laying on her back, with her arms and legs hung over the sides of the massage table. Here, they were tied to the lower shelf where clients would place their belongings. The thing that caught James's attention more than anything else, was Mary, slowly, and delicately lapping at Maggie's pussy.

"Oh, she likes you watching," Mary smirked between

gentle licks. "She was wet before, but now she's practically drooling."

I blinked a few times, before moving closer. Sure enough, there was a little puddle below Maggie's hips. James stared for a moment, before looking up at her face. Now she wasn't watching me, she was blushing furiously. Moving around the table, he gently stroked her face and her eyes locked on me.

"You okay?" James asked.

Maggie huffed through her gag, before squeaking. James caught the movement from Mary as she lifted her tongue away from Maggie's clit.

"You're loving this, aren't you."

"Mmm…"

James just grinned, before gently prying off the tape. Maggie immediately spat out two wads of women's panties and James froze in confusion for a moment.

"One's mine, one's Mary's," Maggie grumbled.

James replied with a grin and a kiss. As he occupied her mouth, he felt Maggie twitch as she moaned. Clearly Mary was increasing her stimulation.

"How long has this been going on?" James asked, leaning back.

"Pretty much th-aaaaah!-this whole time," Maggie gasped as Mary licked her again. "James, please, I need to cum so bad and she won't let me!"

"Revenge is mine!" Mary called, before gently lapping at Maggie's clit again.

"Is this about her making you spit my cum inside her?"

"Yup," Mary grinned as she kissed Maggie's pussy. "I love this cunt, but I love punishing it more."

"Please James?" Maggie begged softly. "Tell her to make me cum, please?"

James grinned and pecked her lips, before turning to

Mary. "When I give the word, I want you to suck her clit until she screams."

Mary grinned and replied by slowly licking Maggie's clit again, while Maggie let out a long, "Nooooooo! So mean!"

James grinned and quickly stripped naked. Ignoring Mary's hungry glare, James moved around to Mary's head. Propped up on the face-rest, James looked underneath and spotted the release pins. Pushing them aside, James lifted Mary's head and slowly removed the entire face-rest, causing her head to swing back under its own weight.

"You're a bad man," Maggie pouted.

James just smiled and pressed his erection to her cheek. "You love me."

Maggie narrowed her eyes, before opening her mouth. James didn't need any more of an invitation to push his cock into her mouth. He didn't go very far, he wasn't trying to choke her. But the shape of her throat was irresistible to touch. Gently holding her chin with his hands, James slid them down her body, feeling the shape of her neck. Then after gently taking hold, James pushed his cock in a little further. Maggie swallowed her saliva around his cock, before James retreated. He could feel her tongue lapping over the head of his cock with each small thrust.

"Can I go deeper?" James asked.

The small bob of Maggie's head made him smile. Pushing his cock further into her mouth, he felt the moment she began to choke and pulled free. Maggie gasped and let out a loud cough, before opening her mouth and sticking out her tongue.

"What, you want me to throat fuck you?"

"Uh huh," Maggie said, not closing her mouth.

James grinned as he teased her lips and tongue with the head of his cock, "Insatiable, pregnant slut."

"Uh huh!" Maggie replied a little louder.

James grinned and slowly pushed his cock into her mouth. Maggie moaned as he got deeper, until he hit the back of her throat, then he retreated. Maggie started making small, 'Ahh,' noises with each thrust and he enjoyed the sensation for several long strokes.

"Oarr!" Maggie managed around his cock on the next retreat.

"More?" He confirmed.

"Uh huh!"

James nodded and stroked the sides of her neck with his hands. He admired the goosebumps that formed under his touch, right before he started pushing in. Like his previous thrusts, she made the 'Ahh,' noise and right at the point where he would have stopped, James felt her swallow. The sensation on the head of his cock made him gasp and without thinking he pushed more of his cock into her mouth. Glancing down, he realised almost his entire cock was in her mouth. He could see the bulge in her throat where his cock was stretching it. Pulling his cock free, Maggie made a small gasp, before closing her lips tightly over his retreating cock. On his next stroke, he went just as far, before looking up at Mary, who was staring at him.

"Ready?"

Mary just smiled and lapped at Maggie's clit. James pulled all the way out, before bending and kissing Maggie softly. She moaned into his mouth for a moment, before James stood up.

"Now."

Mary's mouth latched onto Maggie's clit, at the same time James pushed his cock into her mouth. Maggie's reaction was electric. Her whole body tensed and shook as she strained against the ropes that bound her in place. All she could manage was violent wriggling as James slowly fucked her throat. He cupped the back of her head, holding her steady as he thrust in and out of her mouth. Maggie on the edge of release for so long, started crying out in pleasure. But James muffled her with his cock. When he felt teeth as she did start to squeal, James retreated, letting Maggie scream her tormented pleasure. And like she was instructed, Mary released her sensitive clit and stood up.

James bent down and kissed Maggie softly as she calmed and was relieved when he saw the wide smile plastered across her face. "Did you enjoy that?" He asked with a smirk.

Maggie smiled as drool ran down her face and nodded slowly, "Can you fuck me now, please?"

James snorted and kissed her softly. Standing up, he made sure to drag his dripping erection across her cheek as he turned. Mary slipped off the table and looked nervous for a moment.

"What?" James asked.

Mary bit her lip, "I don't know what I want."

James smirked, "Go get your clit licked for a while, I have a helpless pussy to fuck."

"Yeeees!" Maggie cried from her limp position.

Mary grinned and moved up, while James moved down. Climbing onto the table, James looked down at Maggie's pussy. It looked almost raw, as it drooled onto the table. A soft gasp caught his attention and he looked up at Mary, who was gripping the edges of the table. James could see Maggie's tongue slip out from between her lips and Mary's skin as she ground herself into her friend's mouth.

"That's so hot," James groaned.

"She's doing such a good job," Mary grinned as she rocked her hips slowly.

Positioning himself over Maggie, James fit the head of his cock to her opening. He felt her flinch slightly at the contact and grinned as he leaned further over her. James gently took a nipple in his mouth and sucked on the firm nub, as he rocked his hips forward. Maggie hissed through her minis-trations on Mary. James grinned, slowly rocking his hips, driving his cock in and out of Maggie.

"So beautiful," he smiled.

"Isn't she just?" Mary giggled.

James grinned, "I can't wait to see you both, swollen bellies, dripping and horny all the time."

If it wasn't Mary's moan at his words, it was the tight-ening of Maggie's pussy over his cock, that confirmed his thoughts.

"You're both really into the idea of being pregnant, aren't you?"

Mary gasped and James could see the strain on Maggie's throat from where she had suddenly increased the pressure she had on her friend's clit.

"Is that a yes?" James asked.

"I-I think s-so," Mary groaned, squeezing one of her breasts.

"Good," James smiled and lifted himself. Thrusting firmly into Maggie, she tensed against the ropes, but otherwise made no efforts to show discomfort. "Shit, I was just talking dirty about breeding you both over and over again," James smirked. "But seeing how worked up you both are, maybe I really should have you pump out child after child-"

A jet of warm fluid sprayed up from between him and Maggie. Her hips thrashed, only serving to drive herself down on to James's cock. The firm muscular contractions of her pussy over his cock while he kept thrusting drove him over the edge and he started cumming inside her.

"Fuck yes," James grunted. "Feel that? Imagine, a year from now, you've given birth, you're being a good little mommy, and I strap you back down to this table, and fuck you pregnant all over again."

This time the wail came from Mary, who stared at him

with heat as she trembled through an orgasm of her own. It was a soft thump at the door that caught James's attention. Pulling his cock from Maggie's pussy, he made his way to the door. Stepping to one side, he quickly unlocked it and pulled it open.

"I'm sorry!" Henny squeaked.

"What are…" James trailed off, seeing the top button on her pants was undone. If that wasn't enough, there was also a visible wet patch and she was hiding her hand.

"Who is it?" Mary called.

"Henny!" James called back.

"Bring her in!" Maggie groaned.

Henny's eyes went wide, but she didn't struggle as James took her hand and brought her into the room. He quickly checked the halls and confirmed the lights were on dim to signify they had closed and nobody would be around. Closing the door, he locked it and turned back to Henny, who was staring at Mary and Maggie.

"Are they…"

"Yup," James smiled. "You don't have to join them, if you don't want to."

Henny blushed and nodded quickly, before stepping closer anyway. Mary watched the byplay between us and smiled. "If you wanna watch, come stand where I am, it'll give you a good view."

Mary stood and walked around Maggie, whose face was smeared in Mary's juices. As Mary moved around and climbed back on the table, Maggie moaned in delicious agony. Mary bent over her friend, before licking out a glob of James's cum. Showing it to Henny and James, she swallowed and grinned.

"She's… She's with her," Henny mumbled.

"You okay?" James asked cautiously.

"Uh huh," Henny nodded, while staring. "I didn't think…"

"It's okay," James smiled and gave her hand a squeeze. "Nobody's going to force you to do anything you don't want to."

"C-can I watch?"

"Come stand in front of me," Maggie smiled upside down as Mary continued tonguing her folds.

Henny nodded, before nervously moving forward. "Here?"

"Mhm," Maggie wriggled. "That way you can see all the good stuff, but James can still reach me if he wants.

James watched as Henny moved closer, and stood just outside of reach of Maggie's mouth. He on the other hand moved behind Mary, and gently gripped her knees. He wiggled them backward and Mary groaned as she realised what he wanted. Sliding her ass back on the table, she laid flat between Maggie's legs, at the perfect height for James.

James, grinning at the wet mess between Mary's legs, wasted no time in pushing inside her. She was hot, wet and very ready for the firm fucking he gave her. Each thrust of his hips drove her up against Maggie's clit. Maggie moaned and writhed in her bonds, while Henny slowly leaned over to get a better view.

"Take them off," Maggie groaned.

Henny flinched and stepped back, "What?"

"Your pants, take them off. I'll lick you," Maggie started to beg.

"Bitch," Mary grumbled. "You never licked me until we got with James!"

"I said I was sorry!" Maggie whined back. "If I knew how good pussy tasted before, I would have."

James shook his head, "Ladies, don't bicker. You're putting Henny off."

"I..." Henny frowned. "I don't know."

"I'll be gentle," Maggie offered. "If you want, just take your pants off and step up, I'll make you feel good."

James felt a swat on his stomach, and glanced down to see Mary's hand grab her ass cheek and pull wide. James got the hint and started fucking her again. Only now, he watched as Henny nervously started to push down her pants. She seemed to hesitate at her knees, before shoving them the rest of the way down.

"Such a pretty pussy," Maggie groaned.

Henny blushed furiously and lowered her eyes, "Are... Are you sure."

Maggie's only reply was to open her mouth and go, "Ahhh." That at least broke some tension and Henny giggled, before moving forward. "Closer," Maggie requested. Henny shuffled a little, before she made a small gasp. "Yummy," Maggie moaned.

James kept fucking Mary, grunting as he got closer. But it was the look on Henny's face that drew his eye. Henny was clutching the table either side of Maggie's shoulders. Her eyes were closed and her mouth was open in a wide 'O.' He felt a firm prod on his stomach and glanced down at Mary, who gestured for him to stop. Pulling his cock out immediately, he was about to ask if she was okay, when Mary gestured at Henny with one hand. He stood there for a moment, before Mary kicked him in the shin, before pointing again. Stepping around Mary, he focussed on Henny, who was leaning over the table in her pleasure. Her ass stuck out and Maggie was making small content noises from between her legs. Seeing three beautiful, older women eating one another out sent James's blood pressure right up. He'd never been harder.

Slipping in behind Henny, she gasped when she felt his hands, but she went ramrod straight as James pushed his cock into her from behind.

"Oh god, James!" She gasped.

But James paid her no mind, with one hand on her hip and the other on her shoulder, he pushed her back to the position she was in. James could feel the soft touch of Maggie's tongue where his cock vanished into Henny. He grit his teeth at the sensation as he drove himself in and out of her, ignoring the feeling of his balls batting Maggie's face.

"So good!" Henny squealed.

James took her hips in both hands when he felt her legs start to tremble. But he only increased his pace. Slamming his cock in and out of her, Henny let out a loud scream of pleasure as Maggie sucked her clit between her lips. With a snarl, James erupted for the second time. Pumping his seed into Henny, he felt Maggie's tongue start desperately licking around the base of his cock as he leaked out of her. When the stimulation became too much, James took a step back and sighed. Maggie immediately went to work on Henny's pussy, this time digging through for all his cum. And as Henny clutched at the table once again, James felt himself firming up as Mary wiggled her ass where he'd left her.

CHAPTER TEN

James smiled politely as he led the young man out of his office. He offered his hand to shake, and kept the smile in place as the young man fist bumped him instead.

"So when do I start?" He asked.

"We still have to go through the last of the applicants," James replied evenly. "Once we've come to a final decision, we'll let you know."

"Right, right… Cool," he scratched his uneven beard. "I'll be in touch then!"

James kept the smile on his face as the young man pulled down the back of his pants to show his underwear, before strolling out the front door like he owned the place. As soon as he was out of sight, James slumped his shoulders and sighed. Turning, he headed back into the office to see Maggie shredding his resume.

"I didn't want to make it any less obvious about my feelings towards that one," Maggie said.

James nodded and pulled the older woman into a soft kiss. "There was no way I was hiring him. It was bad enough he couldn't keep his eyes off your chest, but I'm not sure I could stand sitting in a room with him for hours."

"You're going to have to pick someone," Maggie sighed.

He went over and looked at the three names on his desk. The only one he felt would be a good fit was a nineteen year old woman with no experience. It would mean getting her trained and that in itself would probably mean hiring someone.

"I'm going to give it the weekend," James sighed. "What have you got on for the rest of the day?"

"Not my underwear, that's for sure," Maggie said softly.

James's head whipped around so fast his neck cracked. He looked over the smartly dressed woman. A simple white blouse, a pencil skirt and her hair done up in a simple bun. The cherry on the cake was the glasses perched on the tip of her nose as she turned and saw the look on his face.

"James?" She asked.

He didn't respond as he walked over and gently palmed her ass through the skirt. Sure enough, he couldn't feel any underwear.

"If you're going to fuck me, the door isn't locked," Maggie trembled slightly.

Grinning, James slipped her skirt up over her hips, confirming she was indeed going commando. "Then I suppose you better stay quiet, or someone might come in."

"James!" She hissed, but her breath caught in the back of her throat.

James grinned, feeling the walls of her already wet pussy sliding over the head of his cock. "You're such a slut," he grinned. "Every time I touch you, you're already wet."

"It's the hormones," Maggie bit her lip as James thrust up into her, going a little deeper with each stroke. "I can't help it."

"You can't help being a slut?" James gasped, before yanking her hips towards him.

Thrusting firmly into her from behind, Maggie was forced to bite one of her fingers to keep quiet. His cock dragged along her front wall with each stroke, stimulating her g-spot directly.

KNOCK KNOCK

"James, I've got-" Sara stopped in the open doorway. She blinked for a moment, before stepping into the room and closing the door behind her. Turning the lock, she smiled. "Continue."

"Feeling a surge of lust at the thought, James began thrusting his hips.

Sara grabbed a chair and hauled it over to them, before taking a seat. "Get your tits out."

James felt Maggie's tunnel clench over his cock as she let out a small moan. She reached up and started undoing the buttons on her top. James held her by the hips and slowly drove himself into her, while pulling her hips back to meet him. The pace he set made it easy for her to concentrate on what she was doing.

"This is fucking hot," Sara grinned, raising her hips to shimmy down her own pants.

Maggie got the last of her buttons undone, before trying to take it off entirely. James stopped her. Sliding his hands up her body, he lifted her bra up and away from her breasts. The thick, soft material bunched up under her chin as her breasts swung gently with each gentle thrust.

"Oh god I'm gonna cum," Maggie whimpered.

Taking her shoulders, James ran his hands down and took hold of her wrists. Her eyes went wide at the knowledge of what he was about to do and she shuffled her feet wider to brace. James used the grip on her wrists as an anchor point to drive himself into her. Each thrust caused a wet slapping sound on her ass and his balls swung forward, bouncing off her clit. As her eyes rolled into the back of her head, she opened her mouth and let out a loud scream. It was swiftly cut off by Sara, who kissed her deeply. The tall, stoic woman thrust her tongue into Maggie's mouth strangling the cry, while she frigged herself furiously.

"WHAT WAS THAT?" Alice asked, pausing at the sound of the muffled scream coming from the closed office door.

"I believe Mr. Kirk may have left a television on," Baal smiled politely.

"I see," Alice said, unsure of the response, or the name.

Baal took a key and looked at both the ladies before him. Ella and Alice. One was considerably older. She was average height, and had a pleasing shape to Baal's eyes. Her silver hair was done up in a perm and her nails were tastefully painted. She had a kind, grandmotherly look about her. The young woman accompanying her was a short redhead with a cautious expression, only a little older than James. And while he was never one to judge, he got the feeling these ladies were here as friends, despite going to a couples suite.

"Now, ladies, I'll just grab that cart. And I'll take you for a tour of the facilities."

"Thank you Baal," Ella smiled widely.

Baal took the cart laden with their baggage, and suppressed the greedy smile threatening to break over his face.

"GOOD GIRL, now rub it all in."

Maggie whimpered and did as Sara asked. After being

fucked to within an inch of her life, James had taken Sara's instructions and cum all over her face and chest. She felt his eyes on her and blushed, even as she rubbed his sperm into her skin. James was about to comment, when he felt his phone buzz in his pocket. Taking it out, he nervously looked at the two semi naked women before him.

"It's my mother," James said quickly, before answering the call.

"James!" Carla said with a smile. "How are things going?"

James turned his back to the ladies, as Maggie bit her lip as she rubbed her breasts. "Good mum, good. Look, can-"

"I'm so glad!" Carla cut him off mid-sentence. "I just wanted to ring and ask if you had a spare suite this weekend you father and I could take?"

James rolled his eyes and sighed, before sitting down at his computer. Opening up the bookings software, there was indeed a suite available. It was a good thing too, as he could see Baal had just checked out the one beside it. Putting in his mothers details, he confirmed the booking and raised the phone to his ear.

"There, booked all weekend, but you'll have to be out Monday morning for the next booking."

"Wonderful," Carla sighed. "Thank you James, I'll see you tomorrow."

"Sure thing mum," James smiled despite himself. "I love you."

"I love you too," she smiled and hung up.

Turning around, James's breath caught in his throat. Maggie was staring at him helplessly. Sara had yanked her blouse down to her wrists, effectively trapping her arms behind her back. She had sat Maggie in her lap and was gently gnawing on her exposed and unprotected neck, while massaging her breasts.

"Sara, what did you want, when you first came in?" James said, ignoring Maggie's pleading gaze.

"Hmmm?" Sara released Maggie's neck, making her gasp. "Oh, that's right, I wanted your input into the new flower arrangements.

"Shall we?" James asked, standing up.

Taking Maggie under the arm, he helped her stand, while she glared at him. James just smiled and leaned in to kiss her. At the last moment, he changed direction and lightly mauled the untouched side of her neck. Grabbing her ass with both hands, James got a good grip and moaned, feeling the wetness between her thighs. Pulling away, Maggie was breathing heavily, so he lightly pecked her lips.

"Ready when you are," Sara smiled, having used the time to get her pants back on.

"After you," Jame smiled.

"I love you so much," Maggie whispered.

James paused, and looked back at her doe eyed expression. This time he gently copped her face while he kissed her. James injected as much love and passion into the kiss as he physically could, before pulling away and smiling.

"I love you too Maggie."

She was still staring at him as James locked and closed the door behind him. He didn't want anyone to walk in while Maggie wasn't dressed. After a tour of the grounds, where they had in fact discussed flowering plants for the winter, James was wearing his 'got my dick sucked' grin as they came back inside. It was mid-afternoon and Mary was chatting with Henny in the dining room.

"Everything okay?" James asked, approaching them both.

Mary beamed him a smile, before pulling James into a kiss. Henny blushed furiously, but collected her own a moment later, despite James still being trapped in Mary's embrace.

"Everything's fine, I just let Henny know one of the guests is a coeliac."

James thought for a moment, "Gluten intolerance?"

"That's right," Mary confirmed.

James nodded and turned to Henny. "Can you set up a bunch of secondary menus? Ones specific for allergies and other dietary requirements. Everyone always complains that the vegetarian options usually suck at restaurants."

"That," Henny nodded, "Actually sounds like a great idea. My old fitness trainer was a vegan, I'm sure she can help."

"Great!" James smiled and kissed her again. After chatting with the three ladies for a time, they all broke off for whatever they needed for the remainder of the afternoon. James was left to wander and decided to mingle with the guests. Heading back outside, there were families and couples all about, as well as many singles. He smiled and chatted with anyone who took an interest in his passing, until he spotted a familiar face.

"James?" Ella asked, putting down her book.

James turned and seated on an empty chair beneath a large tree was a familiar face. "Ella!" James grinned. "I'd remember you anywhere. How are you?"

"I'm fine," she smiled. "What are you doing here?"

"I work here," James said, a little evasively. "Just passing through checking on the guests."

"Lovely," Ella smiled. "I'm here for the weekend with a friend."

"Oh?" James winked. "A friend?"

Ella burst into a fit of giggles, and blushed, before nodding, "Yes indeed, a friend. Speaking of, who's the lovely older gentleman who booked us in?"

"That would be Baal," Jame replied, not knowing anyone else he'd describe as a lovely older gentleman.

"Baal," Ella smiled. "Do you happen to know if he's married?"

Now it was James's turn to smirk, "Y'know, I never thought to ask. But I'll let you know."

"Thank you James," Ella smiled. "Now, better get back to work. I'd hate for whoever's in charge to be anything like Donna."

"The boss is alright," James smiled. "Let me know if you need anything!"

He walked off with a smile and a wave, completely missing Alice who walked up to Ella from the opposite direction.

"This place looks wonderful," Alice smiled, taking a seat beside Ella. "I'm thinking of getting a massage tomorrow, how about you?"

"Oh," Ella smiled. "I think I'm going to be watching the sights."

"Don't go bringing strange men back to the room now!" Alice chastised her with a smile.

"Oh," Ella giggled. "Wouldn't that stir some gossip in the office."

JAMES WAS WONDERING EXACTLY what he'd gotten himself into. Taking a seat at the head of one of the larger tables in the dining room, he looked at the four women waiting for him. Immediately to his left was Mary, beside her sat Henrietta. To his right was Maggie and beside her was Sara. They all smiled sweetly at him as he sat down to eat.

"Good morning," James smiled at Henrietta and Sara.

They both smiled back as Maggie cleared her throat. "James, we have those extra rooms put in your suite."

"They're both welcome, I'm not sure why we're having

this discussion. If we need more room, ask Joseph to come back." The four ladies just stared open mouthed at him. "Or, did I read this wrong?"

"We just weren't sure how you were going to react, all four of us," Mary said softly. "Have you even told your parents?"

"Speaking of," James sighed. "She, along with my father, will be arriving today. They're staying the weekend and I've already told them we need their room Monday."

"You should really tell your mother James," Henny said softly.

"I know," he replied. "I just know she's going to make a scene. She'll think you're all taking advantage of me."

"Well-"

"You cut that out," James narrowed his eyes at Henny. "I helped you because I wanted to. Not because of some obligation and definitely not because we slept together."

Henny sniffed and wiped away a tear, before smiling widely as Mary hugged her. They ate quietly for a moment, while Henny recollected herself and Mary continued.

"I'm thinking with all the extra land we've been purchasing, that we should build a cabin, separate from the spa."

James nodded, "Why separate?"

"Between the five of us, there's no doubt going to be a lot of children running around. Having that many spread over this whole place won't be easy to manage. Not to mention the suite itself can only go so big, unless we build up."

"Alright, talk to Joseph," James smiled at Sara, who grinned back. "In the meantime, what are we doing today?"

"Oh, that's right," Mary piped up, "You and I have a couple's massage at noon."

"Noon," James nodded. "I wonder when my parents are getting here."

Hours later, James checked the clock above the door to

his office. It was almost time to get ready for the massage. Mary had gone off to prepare the room already, while Maggie and Sara had met up with Joseph to talk about construction. Henny as usual was working the kitchens, and she was definitely in her element. With a groan and stretch James shut off his computer and got to his feet. Stepping out of his office, James locked the door and turned, face to face with his beaming mother.

"James!"

He let out a small, "Oof," as she thumped into him, but he hugged her back.

"How are you son?" Matthew asked.

"Good dad," James grinned as Carla loosened her grip. "I was wondering when you were going to arrive."

"We planned on being here for breakfast, but we had a flat battery and needed it replaced," Carla sighed.

"Alright, well I can't see Baal anywhere. So let me take you to your rooms. Have to be quick though," James added. "I've got a massage in a few minutes."

"You're getting a massage?" Matthew raised an eyebrow.

"Giving a massage," James corrected.

"Haven't you got staff for that?" Carla asked as they started walking. "I seem to remember an older woman."

"Yes, that would be Mary," James said, holding back a sigh that threatened to escape. "It's a couple's massage, so unless she grows an extra pair of arms, I need to be in there."

"James," Carla crooned softly. "You know I'm just looking out for you."

"I know, mum," James rolled his eyes. "But one day you'll have to come to the understanding that I'm a grown man."

"Yes but-"

"A grown man who likes putting his penis inside grown women!" James cut her off.

"James!" Carla gasped. "Too much information!"

"Let it go Carla," Matthew grinned. "He's pushing your buttons because you're interfering."

"And why aren't you helping?" Carla grumbled.

"Help with what?" Matthew asked. "As he said, he's a grown man. Either he knows what he's doing and he'll be fine, or he doesn't know what he's doing and he'll learn."

"What if he loses the spa?"

"How on earth would I lose the spa?" James chuckled.

"If you got her pregnant and she sued for custody!"

James stopped in front of the cabin he'd assigned for their stay and unlocked the door. "We'll talk about it later. Here's your key."

"Son-"

"By dad," James turned and walked away.

He shook his head as he heard his fathers voice reiterate, "Grown man!" as the door closed behind him.

With a sigh, he wondered what he should do to placate his mother. Surely there had to be something. She was so hung up about the age difference. Swinging by one of the staff bathrooms, James gave his hands a clean and made sure he was presentable. He was already a couple of minutes late, so a few more to make sure he looked professional wouldn't hurt. Fixing his collar, James gave himself a final check and paused. There was a small grey hair in his fringe, where there wasn't one days earlier. He leaned forward and gripped it. Quickly plucking it out, he tossed it in the bin and headed for the door.

With a sigh, James shook his head to clear the thoughts about the six months of his life that he'd lost. He'd have to be more careful. He made his way to the couples massage room and saw the door was already locked. Giving it a quick knock he slipped in his key and opened the door.

"Oh good, I was wondering where you got to," Mary said

from her position rubbing Ella's back. "I've already applied oil for you."

"Thank you Mary," James smiled.

The tables were side by side with Ella on one and a red-headed woman on the other. Both were nude but their lower bodies were covered by a towel. Mary had a smile on her face as she worked away on the older woman, but something about the redhead made James pause.

"Alice?"

The woman had a sharp intake of air, before sitting up and rolling part way over. James got a good look at his old temporary colleague as her pendulous breasts sat proudly in the open for all to see. A moment later, she blushed as bright as her hair colour and pressed herself back into the table.

"J-James!" She stammered. "What are you doing here?!"

"I work here," James stared at a spot on the floor. "I didn't realise I was here to massage you. I can try and find someone else if you'd be more comfortable."

"Don't be silly," Ella chuckled. "I'm sorry if I've upset you Alice. I met up with James yesterday and made sure to book him for your massage."

"Ella!" Alice snapped, lifting her head, but not her torso.

"It's fine," James smiled politely. "I really can try and find someone else, it's not a big deal."

Alice sighed softly, "No James, it's fine. I just wished some old bitch didn't spring it on me."

Ella snorted and laughed even as Mary tried to hold back her own giggles at the situation. James just rolled his eyes and moved over to Alice. Picking up the oil that had been left out, James applied a little to his hands, before adding just a little more to Alice.

"Anywhere in particular that I should concentrate on?" James asked.

"My upper legs," Alice said softly. "They always get so tight after a week sitting at my desk."

James smiled and nodded to himself, remembering those awful chairs the office used. "I'll take care of you, just relax."

Starting at the shoulders, James ran his hands over her skin. He could feel the tension in small spots, along her spine and neck, but didn't find any major issues. Alice breathed deeply and relaxed as best she could feeling his hands on her. They tickled slightly as his fingers brushed the sides of her ribs, but before it got too bad, he'd already moved on. When his fingers worked into her shoulders, she let out a small moan of pleasure.

"You okay?" James paused. He was sure that was a good moan, but she'd been wary of him not a minute earlier.

"Uh huh," Alice grunted.

James smiled and continued. Alice melted as his hands worked their magic. She'd been so concerned about the pain in her legs, she hadn't noticed the tension in her neck and shoulders. It wasn't bad, but it was enough to give her the smallest of headaches, and feeling it recede was heavenly.

James worked down her body, picking away at every tense muscle as he went. Each time he dug in the palm of his hand, or his fingers, he felt her flesh melt even further. Alice's eyes rolled into the back of her head as he pressed into the globes of her ass. She couldn't help the small kick of her legs from the intense pleasure of his hands. She was in her own little world, right up until he moved onto her legs. She grit her teeth and controlled her breathing. The ball of warmth that blossomed inside her ached for release. James continued, methodically stroking her flesh and stretching her muscles. By the time he got to her feet, Alice was biting her lip and trying desperately to control her trembling.

"Alright, would you like to turn over?" James asked.

Alice blinked and nodded slowly into the face rest, "Ummm, can I have a towel?"

James blushed for a moment and fixed the one draped over her hips. Then he grabbed a spare and laid it over her shoulders. Alice took hold of the towel and rolled, keeping herself hidden from him. James on the other hand, while he may have enjoyed the view, was more concerned about Alice's comfort and turned away until she got comfortable.

"Ready for me to continue?" James asked.

"Please," came the one word reply.

James moved up and Alice looked him in the eye for a moment. She looked nervous but shot him a smile and closed her eyes. James did his best, massaging the front of her shoulders, before moving down onto her chest. He kept the towel in place and was careful not to touch her anywhere inappropriate. This was despite him feeling that was exactly what she wanted. Moving lower, he firmly rubbed the muscles in her stomach, ensuring she was good and comfortable.

But it was as his hands ran down the fronts of her thighs, he felt her suddenly tense. Glancing up, Alice's face was screwed up tightly and her breathing came in fits. Alice had been building to this moment. It was equally the best thing she had ever experienced and the worst. James, the attractive young man she befriended work. The man she'd softly pined for when he left. Had massaged her until limp and the over-whelming pleasure of it all had finally pushed her over the edge. That small ball of heat inside her core finally spilled over.

Clenching her jaw and trying desperately to hold her breath, she came hard and long. To her horror, James seemed to realise what was happening, as his hands stopped on her thighs and lifted away.

"No!" Alice squeaked at the loss of contact.

James just looked from Alice, to Mary, who was staring at Alice as she came on the table. Mary's eyes flicked to James and she grinned, before going back to Ella, who was staring intensely at the ceiling. When Alice finally fell limp, she covered her face with her hands and refused to look at James, who sighed.

"Would you like for me to continue?"

"Okay," Alice said softly.

James nodded and put on a polite smile, while he continued to rub down her legs. He finished up the massage as professionally as he could, before directing Alice to the shower and swiftly left the room. Groaning at the awkwardness of the situation, James found himself stepping under the hot water of his shower, trying to forget the whole thing.

"Who's she to you?" Mary asked, climbing into the shower behind him.

"Old work colleague," James replied. "Worked in an office, she was the receptionist and we chatted a bit."

"So you haven't slept with her?"

"Slept with who?" Maggie asked, stepping into the shower behind Mary.

"Old work colleague, and no," James sighed. "I never slept with her and now she probably hates me. That must have been mortifying for her."

"I don't think it's as bad as you think," Mary smiled and started to scrub his back.

"Oh, what makes you think that?"

"She didn't ask you to stop."

James paused for a moment… But he didn't get hopes up.

"Are you okay?" Ella asked Alice as they got back to the room.

Alice sighed and let her head fall into her hands, "I ruined it, didn't I?"

"I hardly think you're the first woman for that to happen," Ella said softly.

"Really?" Alice asked. "You know any other women who stumble into their old crushes, massage parlor and orgasm on the table? He wouldn't even look at me afterward."

Ella sat beside her and pulled the younger woman into a hug. "I think you'll find, he was nervous about upsetting you, rather than embarrassed by you dear."

"You think?" Alice snorted, not quite believing her.

"Alice, he was more than willing to find someone else to come in and do the massage. If he didn't want to put his hands on you, he could have found someone else."

That at least made her pause. "Do you think so?"

"I'm fairly confident," Ella smiled.

Alice shook her head, "It doesn't matter. What are we doing tonight?"

Ella smiled at the change of subject and patted her hand. "They're running a movie night tonight. Wanna grab a picnic table and eat junk food?"

Alice grinned and nodded, "Actually, that sounds great."

MAGGIE AND MARY had made themselves scarce. James had frowned and tried to argue the point, but realistically, neither of them wanted to deal with his mother. In the end, he'd conceded with a kiss to each of them, before joining with his parents, while she and Mary went to watch the evening movie together. Sara was off spending the night with her father, and Henny was still working the evening shift to cover a staff member who was ill, so the two of them got comfortable on a picnic table. That was until Mary nudged her and pointed to a pair of women sitting a few meters away.

"That's them," Mary whispered.

Maggie glanced over, seeing the older woman, beside the younger redhead. She nodded and glanced at Mary. "She's pretty."

"James totally wants to fuck her."

Maggie smirked and nodded, "I wouldn't mind taking her for a spin myself."

They sat in silence as one of the waiters brought out a bowl of chips for them to share. Henny had clearly snuck in some other treats as well and the two ladies smiled at her thoughtfulness.

"What do you think we should do about James?" Mary asked.

"James's mother, you mean?"

Mary sighed, "Yeah. I mean, I know what this must look like, but I can't imagine how much worse it's going to get when she discovers we're all pregnant."

Maggie glanced over at Alice, who was laughing at something her friend had said, before frowning. "His mother wouldn't have an issue with her."

Mary glanced at her friend and frowned, "She hasn't done anything wrong."

Maggie sighed and nodded, "Sorry. I just worry that James's mother is going to try and interfere."

"Good luck," Mary snorted. "You know the rules, without getting us pregnant, he's going to die. You think he'll walk away from a set of brood mares like us?"

This time Maggie giggled and shook her head, "God, we sound like such sluts."

"And I'll wear that tag with pride, while he fucks me senseless into your tasty little cunt."

Maggie shivered and climbed to her feet. "I'm just going

to pee."

"I'll be here!" Mary called softly.

Maggie quickly made her way to the nearest bathroom. Slipping inside, she lifted her skirt, slipped down her panties and quickly relieved herself. When she was done, and her hands were clean, Maggie stepped out of the room and bumped straight into a familiar face.

"Alice," Maggie gasped.

The younger woman paused nervously, "I'm sorry, have we met?"

Maggie sighed and realised how idiotic it had been to use her name like that. "I'm sorry dear. I'm a friend of James's"

Alice's expression went from mild concern to distress in an instant. She turned on the spot and stormed away. Maggie, realising she's stuck her foot even further into her mouth, went after her.

"Alice! I'm sorry, please talk to me?"

"Why?" Alice snapped. "Clearly you've got some gossip going on in here. What happened to client confidentiality? I should sue this place!"

"I'm sorry," Maggie whispered. "This has all come out so terribly wrong. I'm so terribly sorry. I had no intention of upsetting you."

"No, just invading my privacy? I thought James was better than that."

"He is!" Maggie called, but Alice had already stormed off.

JAMES SIGHED, chewing the final mouthful of what should have been a wonderful pork chop.

"I just don't know why you can't find a nice girl your own age. What about her?"

James turned and saw Alice storming towards him.

Before he could ask what was wrong, she reached out and slapped him.

James was stunned as she stared at him for a moment as tears rolled down her cheeks. Before she turned and stormed back out the way she came.

"What on earth was that about?" Carla demanded.

James just shook his head and stood up. "Thank you for the company, but I think I'm needed elsewhere."

Getting up, he quickly went after the irate redhead. He didn't know what had happened, but if she was hurting, he wanted to know what he could do to help.

"James!" Carla called after him.

CHAPTER ELEVEN

James watched Alice dart into her suite and close the door behind her. Hurrying to catch up, he came to a stop, took a deep breath, and knocked gently.

"Go away James!"

"Alice, please?!" He called out. "I just want to talk!"

"What? So you can feed your little gossip channels even more? No thank you!"

James frowned for a moment, "Gossip channels? What are you talking about?"

"James?" Ella asked, coming down the hall.

"Ella, make him leave!" Alice yelled from inside.

The older woman looked from James, to the door and back. "What happened?"

"Honestly, I have no idea," James sighed. "I was having dinner with my mother-"

The door swung open and Alice, with furious tears rolling down her cheeks, stood in the doorway. "You told your little friends all about what happened in the massage room. You've completely humiliated me and-"

"Alice!" Ella snapped. "How do you know it was him that started the gossip?"

She suddenly got all flustered, but shook her head. "It doesn't matter who it was. I'd like to leave. I'm clearly not welcome here."

"Alice…" Ella frowned

"I'm sorry," James mumbled softly. "I really am. I have no idea what Mary said to you, but I'll be sure to speak with her."

"It wasn't Mary, it was some other woman," Alice snapped. "And do you really think an invasion of my privacy is worth 'speaking to'" She mimed bunny ears with her fingers.

"That would have been Maggie then," James sighed.

"Is there some way to get a refund or something for Ella, seeing as I'm not staying?" Alice harrumphed.

James nodded sadly, "Yeah, I'll sort that out for you now."

"Don't get yourself in trouble on my account," Ella added quickly. "I know it wasn't your fault with Donna, so don't do anything you'll regret."

"Thank you for your concern," James smiled. "But I own the spa. My uncle died and left it to me the day I left."

"So that bitch works for you?" Alice demanded incredulously.

"Alice, I'm sorry about whatever it was that happened," James rounded on her. "I'm trying to be as professional as I can to an old friend of mine who's clearly upset about something I have no knowledge about. But if you call the mother of my child a bitch one more time, I'll have you escorted off the premises!"

"Pregnant?" Alice whimpered.

James saw the broken look on her face and his heart broke. All her strength went out of her. The anger, the frustration and her attitude all broke down as she began to slump to the floor. James darted in, catching her around his waist and after a moment of struggling, she clung to his shirt and balled her eyes out into his shoulder.

"Alice," James said softly as he supported her. "Come on now let's get you into the room where it's quiet."

"Why won't you leave me alone?" She cried, despite gripping his shirt tightly.

James bent and far easier than he thought he could, scooped her into a bridal carry and brought her inside. Ella came in afterwards and closed the door behind her. James carried her into the lounge and took a seat. He had intended to slip her off onto the couch beside him, but Alice simply clung to him instead.

"Alice, please talk to me?"

"I went to pee, and ran into that b… Into Maggie," Alice sniffed and tucked her head against his chest. "She recognised me by name, and when I asked if we'd met, she said she was a friend of yours."

"Maggie is pregnant with my child, she's far more than a friend," James said, regretting it as Alice seemed to become more distraught. "Alice, what's wrong?"

"It's not fair," Alice whimpered. "It's just not fair."

"What's not?" James prodded.

"You, this situation, everything really," Alice trembled and sat up. Shifting onto the couch beside James, she leaned up against him.

"I thought you were gone forever, and then you popped up here. You made me feel things I hadn't in a long time and now I find out you're with another woman who's already pregnant."

"I'm sorry," James said, putting an arm around her.

"Not as sorry as me…" Alice whispered. "You be a good dad James, and I hope she's a good mommy."

The way she said it, rang some warning bells and James glanced at Ella, to see the same worry in her eyes.

"I can't have children James. It's why I don't date. Every guy I meet wants to have kids and start a family and I can't do that." Extra tears rolled down her cheeks. "I was in an accident as a child. My dad was drunk and hit a tree, I suffered severe organ damage and spent a couple years in and out of a hospital. I'm broken James, so when I saw you and you were happy to see me. I got my hopes up, that maybe, just maybe I'd found someone who might look past my brokenness and see me for me. It's all gone so very wrong."

"Alice, do you know about-"

She shoved herself off him, "Just what are you trying to pull, huh?" She looked angry again. "I've read your website! I just opened my heart to you, and you're trying to sell me someth-"

"WOULD YOU SHUT UP!" James snapped, as Alice fell silent. "Please, just listen to me. I know you're upset, I know you're angry and I know you feel betrayed. I don't know what was said about you behind your back, but I'm trying to help you…"

Getting up, James took out his phone and fired off a quick text. As he did so, Alice slipped from the room and relieved herself, while Ella started making coffee.

"I hope you know what you're doing," she said.

James nodded, "I always liked Alice. If I can help I will, but I need proof or you'll both think I'm crazy."

"I already think you're crazy," Ella laughed. "I'll be very disappointed if you hurt her young man."

James nodded in agreement, but was spared from having to respond by a knock on the door. Striding over, he pulled it open and saw Maggie, Mary and Henny all with varying levels of worry on their faces. Maggie clutched the binder with all their medical records to her chest and looked on the verge of tears.

"She hates me, doesn't she?"

James sighed, and gave her a small kiss, "Come on, let's get this straightened out."

Turning around, he saw Alice staring at them all, but she could see Maggie's tears and hesitated.

"I'm sorry," Maggie blubbered. "I didn't mean for it to come out like that. Mary told me you and James knew each other and when I bumped into you, I squeaked out your name. I'm sorry."

Alice seemed to come to a decision and sigh, "Look, whatever it is, you want to tell me. Just get it over with."

Maggie held out the folder and James gently took it, before walking it the final steps to Alice. She looked confused as she took it and opened it up. Turning, she placed it on the bench as Ella moved to stand beside her.

"What is this?" Alice asked.

"They're medical records," Ella said softly. "All of them are about various issues with female infertility. This here," she held up a sheet with Maggie's name at the top. "This procedure was carried out by my husband before he died."

"I'm sorry," Maggie frowned. "Your husband was an excellent surgeon. The scar from the procedure is so faint nowadays."

"Wait, you?" Alice asked. "James said you were pregnant. How can you be pregnant after a hysterectomy?"

"Turn to the back," Maggie smiled uncomfortably under the younger woman's glare.

Alice turned back to the folder, but Ella was quicker, plucking out the documents in the rear.

"I don't..." Ella looked up at us with confusion and handed over the documents to Alice.

Alice spent a few minutes going over it, before turning

back to James. "Okay, so break it down for me. What exactly does all this mean?"

"It means that if you want a child, I have something that can help," James said evenly.

Alice blinked then sighed and put the documents back in the folder. "Just get out James."

With a nod, James turned on the spot and gestured for the three ladies who accompanied him to head out.

"Just who does he think he is, huh?" Alice snorted as her lip trembled.

"What if he's telling the truth?"

Alice snorted and wiped away another stray tear. "He just wants to fuck me. I'm something to be fucked by men. I can't get pregnant, so there's no risk."

"Alice!" Ella snapped. "Get a hold of yourself!"

"What?" Alice snapped back. "That's what he was implying, wasn't it?"

"Of course he was, that's how it works. And did you see the three women who were with him? They're staff, they work here!"

Alice sighed, "What's your point?"

Ella opened up the folder and quickly separated them into piles. "Three records, three women. A hysterectomy, ovarian cancer and a bill for years worth of failed IVF treatments. We know who Maggie and Mary are," she said, tapping their documents. "I'm betting the other is Henrietta."

"Is it possible your husband-"

"Don't finish that sentence please," Ella growled.

Alice dropped her gaze, "Sorry Ella, I just… What do I do with all this information?"

Ella hugged her firmly, before lifting her chin to look her in the eye. "You sleep on it. You take the time to think. You come to a decision, and you base it on your ability to gain happiness. There's no point being rich or successful if you're miserable and lonely."

"So you're saying-"

"I'm saying that he's an attractive young man who clearly likes you. And then there's the possibility that he's telling the truth."

Alice nodded, "I gave up on the idea of being a mother, before I was old enough to understand what that truly meant."

"The decision is yours," Ella smiled. "Now, I'm going to take a shower, and go for a walk."

"A walk?"

Ella smiled mischievously.

James woke, the following morning, to the wonderful sensation of lips wrapped around his cock. Snapping awake, he realised that Maggie and Mary were both still asleep. Glancing down all he could see was a shape under the blanket.

"Good morning," James grunted.

Their lack of reply and sudden deepthroating made it obvious that it was Sara who had slid under the sheets. James laid there, between his three lovers and groaned softly as he filled Sara's mouth. She hummed in appreciation, before lifting off his cock with a small pop. As she crawled up the bed, Mary and Maggie began to make noises. As expected, Sara popped up from under the blanket and rounded on Mary. She kissed the other woman, making Mary moan, before Sara pulled away. She was far more domineering, grabbing Maggie and kissing her.

"Where's mine?" James asked.

Sara released Maggie and smiled. "I had to feed those two first."

"Yummy," Maggie purred.

James grinned as he tasted a bit of himself on her lips. He didn't care.

"Come on," Sara grinned. "Henny's put a big breakfast on."

James grinned as the three ladies got up. They dressed slowly. Being a Sunday, the facility was open, but they had relatively few responsibilities unless something came up. As one, they headed for the dining room and took their seats. It wasn't long before Henny and another waitress came out with their food. James snagged Henny's hip as she walked past and she bent down for a kiss, before straightening and coming to a stop.

"James Kirk!" His mother snapped.

James sighed, and turned to face his parents. His mother looked irate, while his dad gave him a wink that made him feel slightly dirty.

"Just what do you think you're doing?" Carla demanded.

"Kissing a beautiful woman," James said evenly.

"James!" She snapped. "Isn't it bad enough you're sleeping with one of them?"

"One of THEM?" James frowned. "You're talking like they're something other than what they are."

"And what ARE they then? Hmm?"

"Pregnant with my children," James snapped.

Turning his attention back to his food, he ignored the stares he was getting from the four women. Even Henny, as she sat at the table. The waitress quickly scampered away, sensing danger.

"W-which one?" Carla asked softly.

"Which one what, Mum?" James said over his shoulder.

"Which one is pregnant?"

James smirked, "All four of them."

He heard a small giggle, and turned to see his mother's expression. That small giggle turned into a full laugh, but even Jame's father looked concerned. After wiping her eyes, she straightened and shot him a smile. "Good one James. Now, can you ask a couple of your staff to move to a different table. I'd like to sit with my son."

"And I'd like to sit with the women I love!" James snapped again at his mother. "Mum, I love you. I do. But you need to just accept the fact I'm a grown man, who's making his own decisions. Maggie, Mary, Henny and Sara are all pregnant with my children. I'm having a home built on the property for all of us to live together and there isn't a damn thing you or anyone else can do about it. So go find your own table!"

"Carla, go take a seat. Let me talk to him," Matthew said firmly.

James watched his mother grapple with herself for a moment, before storming off and taking a seat on the far side of the room. The few people in attendance quickly looked away from her, but she was oblivious as she stared directly at James.

"Was any of that a lie?" James's father asked.

"Not a word," James said firmly. "You're both going to be grandparents."

"I'm doing some landscaping before the foundations go down for the house next week," Sara said.

"And we will have construction starting up in the next few weeks," Maggie continued.

Matthew just looked at each of the ladies and settled on James. "I'll talk to your mother. But this is probably going to take some time."

"She's got nine months," James frowned.

Matthew smirked for a moment and nodded, "Ladies, please look after my son."

"We do," Maggie grinned, and Matthew blushed.

After breakfast, James's parents left for home. Only his father came to say goodbye, while Carla sat in the car and waited. As James moved around the property, he caught sight of Alice's bright red hair on more than one occasion, but only for a second as she quickly headed in the opposite direction. It was as he strolled through the trees bordering the property, he heard a noise. It sounded like groaning and James was concerned someone had been hurt.

Pushing deeper into the scrub, the sound increased in volume and intensity, "Hello?!" James called out. "Are you okay!?"

He could hear something frantically moving, so James hurried along. He had images of someone getting attacked, or there being wild animals in the area. So as Ella and Baal stepped out of a section of low shrubs, hair a mess and Ella's shirt inside out, James froze.

"James, did you need something?" Baal asked evenly.

James looked from Baal to Ella, who refused to look at him, back to Baal. Turning on the spot, James couldn't help the grin on his face as he called over his shoulder, "Keep it down you pair!"

And like that, life got back to normal. Monday happened and hired equipment arrived for Sara to start clearing some of the land. A surveyor came in to verify it was safe to build at the location and an architect arrived to confirm specifications for the building. All the extra people, along with signing off work permits, approving bookings, massages and even a few clients had James running ragged. He barely had time to run interviews and had considered ringing Clarissa, the nineteen year old without qualifications. Unfortunately, he had nobody to train her and he didn't have time himself. By the following Monday, James was pulling out his hair. After taking Sunday off, there'd been a system glitch and all his emails had tripled. He was having to go through everything in his inbox to sort out what was a duplicate and what he needed to keep. Along with all his usual workload, he was contemplating throwing his computer.

KNOCK KNOCK

"Come in!" James called, turning away from the screen in frustration.

It opened and Maggie came in, along with Alice and Clarissa.

"James, you're needed elsewhere," Maggie said softly. "Alice is here to train Clarissa. Alice will be your assistant, while Clarissa will be taking care of reception. In the meantime, they're going to sort out your emails and use it as a bit of training in the process."

"What?" James blinked at the three women, before locking eyes with Alice.

James was sure he was never going to see her again. She'd left as quickly as she arrived and hadn't given any indication she was ever coming back. Baal, through his new relationship with Ella, let him know she was okay. But was having problems with Donna. So seeing her walk in with Maggie, was a surprise to say the least.

"James, I need you to leave, so I can train our new receptionist," Alice said formally.

James just nodded slowly and got up out of his chair. The women parted for him, Clarissa giving him a small "Thank you for the opportunity," before he escaped.

Not that he went far, simply standing at reception and providing a point of contact for the few people that came and went. When the door to his office opened, Maggie came out and she moved to stand beside him.

"What's going on?"

"She applied for the position," Maggie replied softly. "We've spent a few days talking to her, then I rang and extended the offer to Clarissa."

"Nobody thought to tell me you were hiring her?"

"We weren't sure she was hired at first," Maggie said, handing over a document.

James looked down at the NDA signed with Alice's signature.

The rest of the day was taken with a certain amount of trepidation. Alice and Clarissa refused to allow him back into his office. Alice transferred a few calls to reception, before Clarissa continued for the remainder of the day. And other than a brief moment when they both left for lunch, he hadn't seen them since. So as closing time rolled closer, James jumped as the door opened behind him.

"Now, just remember the basics. Don't get overwhelmed. This isn't a corporate office, nobody expects you to answer the phone within two rings, there's no KPI's and if someone's yelling, hang up," Alice told the younger woman.

"Thank you so much," Clarissa smiled widely. "Will you be here tomorrow?"

Alice paused, before glancing at James. He realised she was looking for his answer, and gave a small nod. "I should be. A few more days like this and you should be fine to start taking over. Most of this job is just smiling and being polite. There's nothing difficult we're doing."

"Right," Clarissa smiled. "In that case, I'll see you both tomorrow. Thank you Alice, and goodnight sir!"

James blinked as the exuberant young woman practically skipped out the front door. He watched her head out to a small car and continued watching until she safely drove away. And in the silence of the reception, he heard the shuffling of shoes on carpet, before a familiar presence moved up beside him. Turning his head, Alice was staring straight out the door where Clarissa left, as a tear slowly trekked down her face.

"I wanted so much to hate you," she said softly. "I wanted to call you every name under the sun. I wanted to pay people to collect every shred of evidence they could. I wanted to bring in lawyers and ruin your entire life, and I almost did it too."

James nodded, and turned to look out into the fading light. "Thank you."

"I didn't stop because of you," Alice sniffed and wiped away her tears as fresh ones formed. "I stopped because Ella said, 'what if?' And the more I thought about it, the more I realised that if I went ahead, I'd never know the truth."

"I see."

"James, I signed that form, not because I wanted a job. But because I'm taking a risk, that you're capable of a miracle."

James smirked and nodded his head, "You really going to lie with a straight face about what it's like working with Donna?"

They stood in silence for a moment, before Alice let out an unladylike snort. Slapping his shoulder, she laughed softly. Turning she sat on the edge of the desk and finally looked him in the eye. "You were the first guy I'd ever met, who used to make me laugh, and not stare at my tits while doing it."

James grinned, "I used to stare at your tits at other times."

"I know," Alice smiled widely. "I noticed after my washing machine broke down, and had to wear that lower cut top in your second week."

"I miss that top," James grinned, then he noticed she was shuffling on the desk. "What are you…"

Alice blushed as her underwear dropped around her ankles. She kicked her legs slowly until they dropped on the floor. "Oh, how clumsy of me."

James looked from the pink lace, to Alice and back, before bending over. Grabbing the small garment, James stood and examined them. They looked new, clean and had an obvious wet patch in the crotch.

"One condition," Alice said softly.

"Let me hear it?"

"If, if all of this is a lie, or it just… Doesn't work. Please just… Love me anyway. Don't just use me, and throw me away like all the others."

Shifting closer, Alice closed her legs firmly, but James wasn't trying to get between them. Taking her shoulders, he cupped the back of her head and pulled her into a kiss. As their lips met, she let out a small muffled squeak. Alice kissed back, mimicking the movement of his lips as they tasted one another. When James pulled away, she tried to follow, but he held firm.

"Do you understand what you're asking for?" James asked.

She nodded, "I want you James. I'll give you all of me if you just love me back. And if you really do have a magic penis, I'm going to demand you use it on me… Frequently."

"You'll be one of-"

"Five," Alice nodded. "I know, I've been speaking to them."

James smirked himself and nodded. Of course she would have. They wouldn't have let her sign that form otherwise.

"And you're sure?"

Alice nodded, "I had a girlfriend in college, things got… A little wild."

If it were possible, James got a little harder hearing that. "So when-"

"Now," Alice interrupted. "Here on the desk."

James blinked and nodded. Alice's legs opened wide and James stepped in close. Kissing her softly, his hands went for the buttons on her blouse. Prying them open, one by one, Alice only got more animated. Kissing firmer, her legs wrapped around the back of his knees. James flicked the last button off and Alice threw her arms back, desperately wriggling it off. James pulled away, before trailing soft kisses across her jaw and down the side of her neck.

"Oh James," Alice moaned.

He nibbled softly on the soft skin of her neck, as he took in her scent. He inhaled her as she trembled. Reaching up, he felt for the bra strap, when Alice made a small noise. Stopping immediately, he pulled away as she smiled.

"Here," she said, reaching for the front clasp and twisting it open.

As her bra fell away from her gorgeous flesh, James kissed her quickly. Then worked back down her neck. This time he didn't stop, working lower with kisses and small bites until he reached her breasts. They were warm, smooth and her nipples stood out proudly. Palming one of her breasts, James felt its heat and weight for a moment, before tasting the other. Alice let out a hiss of pleasure as he suckled against her softly. He'd had a hunch that her desire for children had left her sensitive to nipple play. And as she trembled, he realised how accurate his senses really were.

Reaching lower with both hands, James ran his hands up the sides of her legs. They were smooth, with only the barest stubble from her recent shave. Not that he cared about that as his hands reached the skirt she wore. Without stopping, he pushed them up towards her hips. Alice's breath hitched as she lifted her hips from side to side as James pushed them right up. Without her underwear, she was sitting completely bare assed on the desk.

As Alice wiggled her hips to sit on the edge of the desk, she expected James to spear into her. Instead, he lifted away from her breasts and kissed her gently. She moaned as he pulled away, but yelped in surprise as he lifted one of her legs over his shoulder.

"Oh fuck," Alice gasped.

James grinned as he lapped lightly at her clit. It was

already erect and ready, which made it perfect to torment her. With a leg over his shoulder, she shouldn't pull away or close her legs. Giving him perfect access to her as she drooled over the carpet. Sliding his tongue into her labia he grinned as she reached down and parted them for him. With one hand on each labia, she held herself open, while biting her lip. James looked up at her, and closed his mouth over her clit. Twirling his tongue over the sensitive little nub, Alice frowned slightly in concentration. But when he started to suckle on it, her jaw opened, as her eyes closed. Her legs began to tremble and James prepared himself for her orgasm. So it was a surprise when she suddenly pushed him away.

"No, I want to cum on your dick," she gasped.

James nodded and lowered her leg so he could stand. She was breathing like she'd run a marathon and there was a sheen of sweat on her brow. James lifted his shirt off and tossed it aside, as Alice fumbled with the front of his pants. She shoved them quickly down, before his underwear joined his pants. She froze at the sight of his cock, pointed straight at her.

"I want that in me, now," she growled cutely.

James chuckled softly. Taking his cock in one hand, he stepped forward and pressed his cock between her legs. She was so wet, it felt heavenly as his glans pressed into her impossible softness. He must have enjoyed the feeling for a few moments too long, as he felt Alice's firm grip steer him into position.

"I said now!" She snapped.

James grabbed her and pulled her firmly into a kiss. As their tongues met, James pushed in. Her breathing shuddered for a moment, before her legs tightened around him. If it weren't for her desperate grip pulling him tighter, he may have thought there was a problem. Instead, James rocked his hips back out, before pushing himself back in.

Alice pulled away and had an almost pained look on her face as she met his eyes. "James, I'm going to cum." James smiled and leaned in to kiss her, but she placed a hand on his chest to stall him. "I want you to fuck me hard, and keep fucking me until you fill me up."

"Okay," James nodded.

Reaching down, James gripped her ass and thrust firmly into her. Alice made a small noise, and followed it up with a wide smile. "Like that, but faster."

Grabbing her ass with both hands, he saw the mischievous smile before she wrapped her arms around his shoulders and leaned into him. With a firm hand hold, James started to forcefully thrust into her. Alice began to shudder, before she tilted her head up with the same expression from earlier.

"Cum, you gorgeous slut," James said without thinking.

She sucked in a lungful of air, then began to shudder. The moment her pussy started to throb around him, James grunted and increased his pace. His hips met Alice's with loud wet slaps. She pulled her knees up as her legs trembled. With her hips rocked forward, James was able to slam into her just that little bit deeper.

"That's right," James grunted. "You cum on my cock."

"Yes!" Alice cried out as she shuddered violently.

James grit his teeth as he felt the squeezing and milking sensation of her pussy around his cock. He was so wound up from earlier. Being spoiled for blow jobs during the day, he'd been denied at the front desk and was desperate for his late release.

"You ready," James grunted, slamming his cock into her with all his might. Alice wasn't capable of answering, but nodded. "I'm going to breed you, you're going to have child after child, all the while begging for more of my cock."

"Please!?" Alice whispered loudly.

Slamming himself to the balls inside her, James palmed her jaw and pulled her into a firm kiss. Emptying himself inside her, James felt her shuddering and trembling as she came all over again. The sensation was intense as he poured his seed inside her, but he rocked himself gently against her as she clawed at him desperately.

SIX MONTHS LATER

James stepped out of his office, as Clarissa was shutting down her computer.

"You're still here?" James asked.

"Yeah, just finishing up a few things before the weekend," she smiled.

James just shook his head, "Book yourself in for a massage. I don't pay you to work this hard."

"I actually wanted to ask about that," she said nervously. "Is there some kind of staff discount?"

"Ummm," James scratched his head nervously. He wasn't sure quite what she was about to ask, but she was still only nineteen. "Possibly, what are you looking at?"

"I've been dating this girl for a few months now," James sighed in relief. "And I was wondering if there was a discount on a room for a couple nights."

James nodded and gave her a smile. "Tell you what, I'll comp you a room for a weekend, and if you get married, I want a table near the front."

Clarissa beamed and gave him a small hug, "Thanks James."

"You're welcome, and hey," he smiled. "Don't work too hard. Your loved ones aren't going to wait forever while you work. Better to spend time with who matters, so no more late finishes."

"Like you're one to talk," Clarissa smirked pointing at the clock.

James rolled his eyes, "This is the time I normally finish on a Friday."

"Really?"

"Who do you think locks the front doors?" He chuckled. "Speaking of, staying or going?"

"I'm going, I'm going," Clarissa smiled. She grabbed her handbag and headed for the door with James beside her. When she stepped out, she paused and shot him a smile. "Happy birthday James."

He blinked for a moment and smiled. "Thank you Clarissa." He'd completely forgotten what day it was. Time flies when you're having fun, and having this active a sex life was certainly fun. He was eternally grateful that Clarissa didn't ask questions about the length of his meetings. Though she did politely make a comment about noise, shortly before providing a quote for sound insulation.

James waited long enough to see the young woman climb into her car and start driving, before locking the front doors. They swept through the place every night, and he did so again. The last thing he wanted was for someone to be stuck in the interior for the evening. The restaurant was still open, but with the recent onset of snow, the movie nights had paused. Though there had been a little interest in doing a winter event if the weather was nice enough. Satisfied all was well and where it should be, James gave a lingering look at the hallway that led to his old suite, before heading out the back. Flicking the lock on his exit, James tightened his jacket over himself. The breeze was only slight, but it was cold at this time of day. He was lucky that Sara had set up a temporary path marked with pickets. Now no matter the weather, you had an easy way to make it from the facility to the house and back. And in the summer, it could be taken down to allow foot traffic.

Following along, he made it to the front door and pushed it open. The inside of the cabin was beautiful. It was built of logs to match the smaller cabins in the area. The wood was harvested from the surrounding land. The areas that were cleared were used to put biking and walking trails for the exercise enthusiasts that came up. Inside, however, it was anything but a draughty cabin. The heater was on, the first floor smelled like dinner was cooking. The TV was on, but muted and there was no sign of any of the ladies.

With a shake of his head, James headed towards the stairs, and saw a pair of women's underwear. Frowning, he bent and picked them up. He wasn't sure which of them had dropped these, but as he put his foot on the first step, he spotted a second. Halfway up the stairs was the third and by the fourth at the top James was curious about what was going on. The fifth and final pair of underwear were hanging over the doorknob to the master bedroom. And stuck to the door itself, was the words:

OPEN FOR BIRTHDAY GIFTS

With a grin, James slipped the panties off the doorknob and quietly opened it, only to freeze in place. There were five pantiless asses pointing at him from the bed. Each of them was completely naked except for a waist garter, thigh high suspenders and a pair of heels. Each of them had nice swollen bellies and I could see from here they glistened between their thighs.

"Waiting for someone?" James asked casually.

A series of small giggles rang out, and James grinned as he stripped off his clothes. With his erection leading the way,

James strode up to the five of them and palmed their asses. Under his touch, each of them squirmed, but James moved from one to the next. The first in silver heels was Sara. Pregnant with a daughter, James watched as she stroked her stomach while grinning at him. The next in line wearing purple heels was Maggie pregnant with a son. He grinned at her, seeing a small gag had been fitted in her mouth while she stared at him lasciviously. Beside her, as always was Mary in a familiar pair of red heels. She was also pregnant with a son and laid her head comfortably on her arms and smiled softly at him.

Beside her was Henny in a blue set of heels. She had decided she didn't want to know the gender and James had agreed with her request. All he could see of her was the blush that ran past her shoulders, but the sticky mess between her legs told him she was no less keen for her attention. And last, in a pair of black heels, was Alice. Despite being the latest to fall pregnant, her belly was the largest containing a set of twin girls. Being pregnant had affected them all deeply, but Alice had long since designated herself 'James' personal cumslut.' He had to start leaving his office door open to dissuade her from stripping naked and begging for sex multiple times a day. She was openly staring while mouthing the word, "Please," over and over again.

Bending over, James ran his tongue from her clit to her asshole. Alice let out a long soft moan of pleasure. James moaned at the taste of her and licked again. Alice trembled in place as James lapped at her pussy and clit in equal measure. It was as he sucked the firm little love button into his mouth, she broke composure.

"Oh fuck, James!"

He just ignored her and lightly brushed his teeth over her clit. It set her off immediately and James gripped her ass to hold her in place as he watched her pussy muscles clench and release before his eyes. Lightening his approach, Alice moaned and gasped for several long moments while he milked her pleasure. As she calmed, he pulled away and swatted her ass.

"Slut," he grinned.

"Your slut," she shot back.

She'd been hopeful but aloof until the day she randomly started vomiting. After peeing on a stick and seeing two lines, she'd then spent a full day crying and clinging to James. Then promptly dedicated herself to being impaled on his cock whenever possible. So as James stepped away, taking said cock with him, she literally growled. But James wasn't going far.

Turning, Henny arched her back with a soft gasp as James speared his cock into her. Putting one leg on the side of the bed, James was able to step up and reach Henny's face. Gently cupping her cheek, James thrust slowly into her from behind. He lifted and turned her head to face him. He kissed her as she moaned in pleasure, unresisting to his demands.

"I hate it when you do this to me," she whimpered.

"Do you really?" James asked, kissing her again. "I think you get off on being embarrassed in front of everyone."

His assumption was answered as her pussy began to clench rhythmically over his cock as her eyes rolled back into her head. James kept thrusting for a few more moments until Henny started going slack. Slowing his pace, James pulled her close and kissed her gently as she smiled doe eyed at him.

"I love you Henny. We all do."

"I love you too," she whimpered as James pulled himself out of her.

"Hey!" Alice complained loudly as James turned away.

Striding right to the front of the queue, he palmed Sara's

ass. "Not often you let me be on top," he grinned and slapped his cock on her ass cheek.

"Don't get used to it," she smirked at him. "Six weeks after Caleb is born, I'm getting myself pregnant again."

James just blinked at her, before taking his cock and pushing it inside her. Even in her heavily pregnant state, she couldn't resist rocking her hips back against him. She physically couldn't just lay there and take it. And even then she still usually preferred to be on top. So slowly fucking her from behind was a rare treat that James savoured.

"I'll admit it's a nice pace feeling that cock slide up inside me, while doing minimal work," Sara grunted.

"All you have to do is ask," James grinned, thrusting his hips into hers.

"Pfft," Sara grinned. "I'm not a cock hungry slut like Alice."

James swatted her ass making her squeak and pull away. James grabbed her hips and pulled her back onto his cock again. "Don't pretend you're not as hungry for my cock as everyone else. You just hide it better."

The soft giggles that went off to James's right weren't argued against. Instead he felt her fingers as she touched herself around James cock. He grinned, feeling her fingers shift and start moving faster.

"See," James crooned. "Just as desperate to cum on my cock."

Sara let out a long groan as her tunnel began to spasm. James knew what she liked and sped up, fucking her harder. In no time at all, she began to tremble and James fucked her with long deep strokes as she climaxed. Pulling his cock free, James stepped back and admired all the asses presented to him. Stepping up, he grabbed Mary's hips, but paused when she shook her head.

"Do me last," she whispered.

James was about to ask why, when she reached up and slid the tip of one of her fingers around her ass, that James realised glistened with lubricant. With a grin, James grabbed Maggie's hips and slowly dragged her ass towards himself, impaling her on his cock.

"Oh, huck," Maggie groaned through the gag.

"First pregnancy," James grinned. "How's it feel to be the first slut to cum on this dick while it bred you?"

James ignored her incoherent babbling as she came around his cock. He had no intentions of stopping immediately as he continued fucking her right through her orgasm. This drove Maggie straight into her second, which prompted her to twist around to stare at him. James just smiled cruelly, not relenting until she started babbling as she came for the third time. Pulling himself free, Alice was practically vibrating from excitement.

Shifting up behind her, James roughly gripped her ass in both hands and slid his cock half way inside her. Repositioning for comfort, he released her and stood still.

"James?"

"Mhm?"

"Oh you bastard," Alice grinned and started rocking back and forth.

"Earn it, slut," James smiled down at her.

Alice gasped and started rolling her hips with each backward thrust. "I ALWAYS earn it!"

"Exactly," James grinned.

Her pussy was exquisite, sliding over his cock. James loved to watch her labia stretch over his length and from his viewpoint he had quite a show.

"James?" She grunted.

"Yeah Alice?"

"James I'm gonna cum."

James just smiled, "Go on then slut."

She whimpered for a moment. James knew exactly what she meant. "James, please?"

"Please what?"

"Please James, fuck your slut while she cums on your dick!" He ignored her for a few moments as she began to tremble. "JAMES!"

Gripping her hips tightly, James thrust himself to the hilt inside her. Immediately he felt her pussy clench in orgasm. Drawing his cock out, James slid it back inside and fucked her slowly, but deeply through her orgasm. Alice for that matter, cried out in pleasure as her pussy gushed fluid over his balls. That only spurred him on and he increased the pace until Alice could do little more than tremble and whine. When he felt her begin to slack, James yanked himself free, before helping her lay on her side. She trembled and heaved large breaths of air, but the wide smile on her face told him everything he needed to know.

"That's a good little slut," James whispered, leaning over to kiss her.

Standing back up, she still pouted, despite her legs no longer supporting her. James just grinned, knowing full well she could live the rest of her days happily being fucked into oblivion. But for now, he had one more of his loves to take care of.

Stepping up behind Mary, she laid forward and pulled her ass cheeks open. James just blinked at her as she acted less like a dignified professional she was outside these walls, and more like a pornstar from a website he hadn't visited in over six months. Angling his cock, James slid it partially into her pussy.

"James!" Mary grumbled.

"Just making sure I'm good and lubricated," he smirked.

Mary rolled her eyes, but enjoyed the sensation of him fucking her for a short while longer. When she made an impatient sound, James pulled free and pressed his cock to her asshole. With a small nudge he felt her ass open, but he didn't push in straight away. He knew that Mary hadn't been a regular hand at anal, so he took his time, and her smile told him it was the right decision. Pressing a little more with each thrust, he got further and further until eventually, the head of his cock slipped past the ring of muscle.

"Oh, fuck yes," Mary groaned.

"That's hot," Alice said.

James smirked, not having realised she had sat up to watch. Henny was quietly masturbating as she watched on from the bed. Maggie was pinned beneath Sara who kissed her furiously, while driving her fingers between the submissive woman's thighs. James just grinned at the sights before him and pushed in a little more. He took his time as Mary moaned with each thrust. He went deeper over time and soon she began to push herself back to accept more of him with each thrust. Until finally James was smoothly fucking his entire length into her ass.

"Fuck, anal never felt so good until you had me," Mary groaned.

"I wanna try that next," Alice pouted. "It's not fair he gets to fuck your ass."

"God, you're such a greedy slut," Henny snapped.

We all paused to look at her and she blushed furiously realising she said it out loud. The next thing out of her mouth was a squeak as Alice dived between her legs. Henny flopped back and gripped the pillows with both hands as Alice treated her clit like a drinking straw. James turned his attention back to Mary and fucked her much harder than he had before. He treated it like her pussy and Mary let out a long cry as her bowels throbbed in orgasm.

"Fill my ass, please!" Mary begged.

"You want me to cum in your ass?"

"Please?!"

James grit his teeth and yanked on her hips as he fucked her from behind. Anal was one thing, but she was over eight months pregnant and he was slamming into her with all his might. As she cried out again in orgasm, James hilted himself inside her and started cumming. His cock throbbed and James gripped Mary's hips almost painfully tight as she rocked and milked his orgasm. With a final grunt, James pulled free and watched the white mess pour out of her.

"Oh fuck," Mary trembled, as Henny let out a long keening cry.

Hours later, the six of them settled on the couch in front of the idiot box after a team effort of scrubbing the kitchen.

"James, your mother," Maggie started.

"I thought she got over it," He sighed. "What's she done now?"

"Nothing," Maggie said softly. "But, she made a good point the other day."

"Which is?"

"That while we're all your lovers, and we all consider ourselves married. A real wedding might cement her affection towards our children," Maggie said evenly.

James frowned, "No, I can't. Asking me to choose to marry just one of you isn't something I want to do."

What he wasn't expecting was for four smiles to light up the room. Everyone except James and Alice, who looked at each other in confusion.

"I'm sold," Sara nodded.

"I agree," Henny nodded.

"Agreed," Mary smiled.

"Well unless someone has some serious concerns, James. We want you to legally marry Alice."

"WHAT?!" The younger woman practically screamed.

James just stared dumbly at each of them, until Maggie smiled and moved to take both their hands.

"Listen, what we have isn't unique. But it is unconventional. Inside this place and especially within our home, we live all as one family. Out there, in the real world, where your mother, and James's mother exist, what we are isn't widely accepted."

"B-but why me?"

"You're his age, attractive and had a thing for him even before we did," Sara snorted.

Alice burst into tears and looked like she wanted to run away. But James was quicker, quickly pulling her into his arms. He held her against himself for several long minutes until she surprisingly drifted to sleep in his arms. When the soft snores filled the room, James smiled and turned to Maggie.

"One condition," he said softly.

"Oh?"

"I want a civil ceremony. One with each of you. Rings, flowers, dresses, the lot. I don't care what everyone thinks, we'll do it here on the premises."

She blinked and smiled as a few tears rolled down her cheeks. James spotted similar expressions from Mary, Henny and surprisingly even Sara, though she glared at him when he caught her trying to wipe them away.

A soft snore caught all their attention as Alice mumbled, "I'm your slut," softly in her sleep.

Hello, and thank you for reading my book. Independent authors like myself live and die by our ratings, from wonderful readers such as yourself.

So please,
   If you enjoyed this story, give it 5 stars and drop a review. Even the words "Good job" will help tremendously.

All the best
   Monty

Hell

Adult LitRPG adventure with plenty of steamy action.

Meet Ryan... That's pretty much about it.

Several thousand people find themselves trapped in a dystopian future Earth. No memories, no clothes and right in the middle of a swarm of monstrosities. But as time goes on, and the true face of humanity is revealed, are the creatures that stalk the night the danger? Or the protection from man's far more vicious adversary... Itself.

WARNING: Contains, a harem, mf, mff, gore, violence, mentioned (but not described) rape and sexual assault, death, did I mention violence? People torn apart by animals and a guy who just wants to keep those closest to him safe.

https://www.amazon.com/gp/product/B08WRLS5PW

The Beast: Trolling In Paradise

Living the dream, a troll-human hybrid works as a gatekeeper for a goblin horde.

At least, that was until a hunting party stumbled across a patrol of elves.

When everything goes wrong, a bright spark leads the way to the future, and maybe even love.

Join Frelser and his wives as they battle goblins, trolls and giant wolves.

Story contains violence, consumption of wizards named Henry, consumption of an elf, a harem, sexy elfin wives, a part orc, a full orc, a succubus and a whole lot of adult entertainment. This story isn't for kids and isn't for anyone squeamish.

The Leader: Trolling In Paradise

The battle with the goblin horde brought prosperity to the town. But under our newfound peace, lies an obvious threat. When the king of the elfs gets word of Frelser and his wives, he sets out to reclaim what he lost.

Read this next installment to discover love, loss and a deep hunger for elf flesh.

Story contains violence, consumption of elfs, a harem, sexy elfin wives, a part orc, a full orc, a succubus (and maybe a few more) and a whole lot of adult entertainment. This story isn't for kids and isn't for anyone squeamish. And hey, if you read the first one, you know what to expect. It's not getting any better.

Rose: A Hucow Story

Outside every major city in Australia, is the beauty of the rugged bush.

But in such open wilderness, there can be far worse.

When a retired member of the special forces takes a trip out bush and stumbles across a pair of sex traffickers, the once broken soldier finds his purpose.

With lust comes love and when the ladies aren't all that they seem, will one man be enough to expose an underground genetic experiment?

Contains a harem, hucows, lactation, MF, MFF, MFFF, MFFF-y'know what, you get the picture. Also contains violence, murder, desecration of a corpse, sodomy of a slave owner with an oversized love toy and many grateful slaves, desperate to thank their rescuer.

https://www.amazon.com/gp/product/B09CF5PJL4

Misery Breeds Company

A battered wife.

A worried neighbour.

A chance at rebuilding the future.

With the death of an abuser, a friendship is born. The quiet neighbour takes the first tentative steps to help the woman of his dreams. But will his failure to admit his feelings out loud, drive her away for good? After all, Misery Breeds Company.

Disclaimer: Non-standard erotic romance tale. Contains explicit sex, domestic abuse (and subsequent recovery), MF & MFF. If you've read my work before, you know what you're getting yourself into.

https://www.amazon.com/gp/product/B08YYLHXNS

The Newest Generation: Fut Files

Ever wonder what it would be like to wake up one day with a ten-inch additional appendage?

Amber sure didn't. But when that new addition lands her in a sticky situation with her spank bank, and best friend, Jane... Well... What's a newly emerged futa to do?

But not everyone's happy with the situation. And someone may be willing to try a permanent solution to end it, before it has a chance to really start.

Welcome to the Newest Generation!

Contains futa, futa on girl, futa on futa, futa on futa on girl. Violence, cheating, minor gore and a f-boi name Dean who just doesn't get it.

https://www.amazon.com/gp/product/B09CNV5TWL

Curse Of Rage

The last, hunted, descendants of an ancient race live a quiet, solitary existence.

When their location is found and a freak accident exposes them to danger, a young man's life is permanently destroyed in the worst way imaginable. Seeking protection amongst those who do not trust him, friends are made and lost.

But with the possibility of love, will the Curse of Rage be quenched in the arms of a broken beauty?

https://www.amazon.com/gp/product/B08LQN3Z65